"YOU USED ME!" HE RAGED.

"Now wait just a minute. A man who uses women then tosses them aside is hardly in the position to point a finger at anyone."

"I'll show you how it feels to be used. I'm an expert. I've been used by the best in the business: agents, business managers, fans. You want an example of what it's like to be used!"

Billy pushed her on her back as Christine struggled to free herself. "Don't do this, please. You can't use me this way!"

He threw his head back and gave a harsh, grating laugh. "That's my line. You haven't been used *yet!*"

CANDLELIGHT ECSTASY ROMANCES®

346 A TASTE OF HEAVEN, *Samantha Hughes*
347 HOPELESSLY DEVOTED, *Alexis Hill Jordan*
348 STEAL A RAINBOW, *Sue Gross*
349 SCARLET MEMORIES, *Betty Henrichs*
350 SPITFIRE, *Lori Copeland*
351 SO DEAR TO MY HEART, *Dorothy Ann Bernard*
352 IN DEFENSE OF PASSION, *Kit Daley*
353 NIGHTSONG, *Karen Whittenburg*
354 SECRET INTENTIONS, *Jean Hager*
355 CALLING THE SHOTS, *Kathy Alerding*
356 A PRIVATE AFFAIR, *Kathy Clark*
357 WALKING ON AIR, *Michele Robbe*
358 RELENTLESS PURSUIT, *Eleanor Woods*
359 SENSUOUS ANGEL, *Heather Graham*
360 WORDS FROM THE HEART, *Natalie Stone*
361 INTERIOR DESIGNS, *Carla Neggers*
362 TOMORROW AND ALWAYS, *Nona Gamel*
363 STAND-IN LOVER, *Barbara Andrews*
364 TENDER GUARDIAN, *Cathie Linz*
365 THE TEMPTRESS TOUCH, *Lori Herter*
366 FOREST OF DREAMS, *Melanie Catley*
367 PERFECT ILLUSIONS, *Paula Hamilton*
368 BIRDS OF A FEATHER, *Linda Randall Wisdom*
369 LOST IN LOVE, *Alison Tyler*

GLITTERING PROMISES

Anna Hudson

A CANDLELIGHT ECSTASY ROMANCE®

Published by
Dell Publishing Co., Inc.
1 Dag Hammarskjold Plaza
New York, New York 10017

To Lydia E. Paglio, an editor who understands, cares, and inspires authors.

Copyright © 1985 by JoAnn Algermissen

All rights reserved. No part of this book may be reproduced or transmitted in any form or by any means, electronic or mechanical, including photocopying, recording or by any information storage and retrieval system, without the written permission of the Publisher, except where permitted by law.

Dell ® TM 681510, Dell Publishing Co., Inc.

Candlelight Ecstasy Romance®, 1,203,540, is a registered trademark of Dell Publishing Co., Inc., New York, New York.

ISBN: 0-440-12861-7

Printed in the United States of America

First printing—October 1985

To Our Readers:

We have been delighted with your enthusiastic response to Candlelight Ecstasy Romances®, and we thank you for the interest you have shown in this exciting series.

In the upcoming months we will continue to present the distinctive sensuous love stories you have come to expect only from Ecstasy. We look forward to bringing you many more books from your favorite authors and also the very finest work from new authors of contemporary romantic fiction.

As always, we are striving to present the unique, absorbing love stories that you enjoy most—books that are more than ordinary romance. Your suggestions and comments are always welcome. Please write to us at the address below.

> Sincerely,
>
> The Editors
> Candlelight Romances
> 1 Dag Hammarskjold Plaza
> New York, New York 10017

CHAPTER ONE

"Get Rich Quick . . . Write a Romance Novel."

Christine Mc Mahon dropped the latest issue of *Women* next to a paperback book on the coffee table.

Why not? she mused, inspired by the multitude of similar articles she had read on the same topic. An English teacher should be able to string a few words together and come up with a salable manuscript. Tapping her tanned cheek thoughtfully she wondered how sensuous she could make the novel without being fired. Schoolteachers weren't supposed to think wicked thoughts, much less publish them for the whole world to read!

Her dark eyes sparkled as they wavered between the cover of *Women* magazine and the bold, eye-catching title of the paperback book: *How to Pick Up a Man*.

Her twin sister, Janelle, who was still in bed, had purchased a book that was of interest to both of them. Maybe, Christine thought, she should forget about writing a romance novel and instead write an instructional manual on how to meet, mate, and marry—not necessarily in that order—a dream man. A spoof! Wouldn't that sort of book appeal to more women than a sweet romance?

With three months of uninterrupted vacation time stretching out in front of them, she and Janelle could wisely use the time off to their mutual financial advantage. Christine closed her eyes, adding another item to her positive-thinking list: The Mc Mahon sisters coauthor a best-selling humorous meet-and-mate book.

Selling the book shouldn't be a problem, not with David, their brother, who was a talent agent, representing them. With Janelle cowriting the book, and David agenting the manuscript, how could they fail? This would be a Mc Mahon family project! Christine could almost visualize a signed contract from a prestigious publishing house being delivered by a Wells Fargo armored truck along with piles and piles of lovely, lovely money.

"Looks good," she said aloud. "Better than good . . . it's a great idea!"

Christine couldn't wait for Janelle to wake up. Gracefully rising, she crossed the pale blue carpeted floor and headed into her sister's room. The toughest part of her bright idea would be convincing her sister to give up her plans to hide out for the summer in the nearby Rocky Mountains.

The way my sister looks, she should be hunt-

ing men instead of deer, Christine mused as she watched the slow rise and fall of Janelle's chest. No doubt, between the two of them, it would be Janelle who'd test out any hypotheses they concocted. Sucking her stomach in, Christine quickly perused her own ample curves.

Pleasingly plump, she observed with a grimace. Her brown eyes swept over her sister's slender form. How could twins look so different? Not only was Janelle tall and thin, she had gorgeous long blond hair and sky-blue eyes. Definitely an exotic bird. *And then there's me,* she thought, *the wren: dark-haired, dark-eyed, and . . . plump.*

Years ago Christine had given up resenting her sister. What was the point? A biological twist of fate had painted their shapes with different brushstrokes. Besides, it was difficult to be envious of someone who didn't have a mean bone in her body. Janelle could have lorded over her less attractive twin, but she didn't. Many times Janelle had refused social engagements because Christine hadn't been invited. The exotic bird protected the wren like a zealous mother hen.

But Janelle carried the devoted-sister routine to extremes. *How to Pick Up a Man* had been a gift for Christine. At twenty-eight, Janelle decided they both had played the field long enough, and they needed to get serious about meeting suitable spouse material. Teaching in the public school system limited their access to available males. Most of the male members of the faculty were married, and the remainder were too young or too boring. Of course, what Janelle was subtly trying to say was that the bird of paradise wasn't going to get serious about any man until she had her more drably plumaged sister firmly ensconced in a safe nest.

Again, Christine's ideas merged. What if she could convince Janelle that she needed her help to catch a man? What if she told her they should organize their manhunt in a methodical manner . . . and write it down on paper!

Brilliant, she congratulated herself. Sweet Janelle Mc Mahon wouldn't consider hunting a man the way she stalked wild animals, but what if she were the bait in the trap? The scheme might work if she could convince Janelle she'd be absolutely despondent staying home alone all summer while Janelle retreated to their cabin hideaway. A few tears shed at the appropriate moment would help. Christine shook her head. Forget the tears. Neither one of them had shed a tear since the tragic death of their parents in a car accident. Basically honest, Christine felt she could twist the truth a mite, but never flagrantly lie.

"Quit biting your fingernails," Janelle requested in a sleepy voice.

Christine jumped guiltily.

"Uh-oh. Something tells me you've been standing at the foot of my bed hatching one of your harebrained ideas." Laughing, never grumpy in the morning, Janelle swung the bedcovers back. "What get-rich-quick scheme are you plotting now?"

"What do you mean?" Christine inquired defensively as she flopped down in the velvet wingback chair beside the dresser.

"We're six weeks away from summer vacation. For the past seven summers you've come up with some wild scheme to make us filthy rich by fall." Her slender hand waved toward the calendar on the desk that she used to jot down appointments. "Look around the end of April of last year if you don't believe me. That's when you came up with the brilliant idea to take our savings and buy an old house to renovate."

Christine smiled. "Yeah, but we doubled our bank account last fall when we sold the house."

"True, true," Janelle groaned, realizing she had reinforced any bizarre idea her twin had in mind. "I also remember you smashing every finger on both hands . . . not to mention the broken arm from falling off the ladder. Or how about the water fountain you created when you decided you wouldn't hire a plumber to redo the plumbing."

"We're all entitled to one or two mistakes," Christine protested with a giggle.

Janelle placed her hands on her hips, tossing her long hair over her shoulder. "How about mistake number two? Was that when you decided the college boy would paint the house for less if I'd go out with him?"

"He did reduce his price."

"Yeah! When you threatened him with attempted rape charges!" Janelle shook her head vehemently. "What about the year before last?"

"Now, now, Janelle, I know you're a history teacher, but can the postmortems, okay?"

"Well phrased for an English teacher. Postmortem. How I ever let you talk me into doing flower arrangements for weddings and funerals, I'll never know." Janelle covered her mouth to restrain a giggle. It really hadn't been Christine's fault the funeral wreath had been delivered to the wrong church. Fortunately she had been able to get the bridal bouquets to the church before the marriage ceremony started.

"*This* idea is foolproof!"

"In the spring *every* idea is foolproof. In the fall I return to my classroom grateful the school board hasn't heard about our summer moonlighting. Not this year, though. I've made my plans for the summer. You're welcome to come along, but unless you've figured out a way to cut down the trees and market them, I'm graciously refusing your kind offer . . . whatever it is."

Christine groaned aloud. "You're only mentioning the tree idea because you know I've already checked it out. Too isolated to make it profitable."

"Thank God. You'd probably amputate your arm with a buzz saw if it weren't. Where you get this materialistic streak from, I don't know.

It's not like we starved as children, or are now living in the slums of Denver."

Christine got up and walked toward the door. There was a time to fight and a time to retreat and regroup her forces. Janelle could be stubborn. It was pointless to pursue the matter when she had decided to be contrary.

"Oh, no, you don't," Janelle protested, grabbing Christine's sleeve. "You aren't stepping out of this room until I find out what you're plotting. I'll be as skittish as a deer the day before hunting season if I let you get out of here without telling me what you're up to."

"Don't end a sentence with a dangling preposition," Christine corrected in an effort to be evasive.

"Better to have a dangling preposition than find myself dangling from the end of a hangman's noose in front of the administration building. 'Fess up, sister dear."

"This time it's a surefire idea . . . and harmless!"

Janelle clapped her hands to her head. "That's what I heard the year you wanted to open a male striptease joint. Now I'm really worried."

"You're the one who restricted my ideas to meeting men that summer."

"I believe I suggested we find summer employment where suitable men would be working."

"My idea wasn't bad, just premature. Denver wasn't ready then, but now . . . that new place, Cheeks, is making somebody into a millionaire. Anyway, what I'm planning for this summer can be done anywhere."

Janelle sank onto her unmade bed. "You're going to open a bordello, right?"

"Janelle! Really! Would I do something like that?" Christine giggled.

"Forget trying to sidetrack me. You're cooking up some nefarious plot with every intention of getting me involved, and I want to know what it is."

"Let's write a book this summer," Christine blurted out.

"A children's book?" Janelle straightened. Secretly she had considered writing teenage adventure stories using her love of the mountains as a base. "I hate to admit this, but I've considered the same idea. Maybe our being twins—"

"Great minds on the same track?" Encouraged by her sister's interest, Christine bounded over and plopped on the bed beside her. "Authors are rich, aren't they?"

"Don't you think we ought to sell the book before we start counting our money?" Janelle teased. "Lots of people have stacks of unmarketed children's stories."

"Children's stories? Who's talking about children's stories?"

Blue eyes glared into brown.

"Jackie Collins already has a monopoly on the type of book you'd like to write," Janelle said disparagingly.

"Our book won't be fictitious."

"Forget it. Masters and Johnson have already written the book you have in mind." Reaching over to the dresser, Janelle picked up her brush and began unsnarling the tangles in her long hair.

Anytime Janelle started brushing her hair, Christine knew she was being subtly dismissed. Only in this case it was more as if Janelle were shouting "Get the hell out of here!"

"You're missing your big chance," Christine warned. "And you're making me miss mine."

Janelle brushed harder.

"I'm suggesting writing a book like the ones you read."

"A historical romance? Forget it. The book racks are flooded with them. Besides, you said fact . . . not fiction."

"I meant a book about hunting!"

The brushstrokes slowed, then halted. "That might not be a bad idea. Sort of a woman's approach to survival in the woods. We could do a chapter on setting up camp, recognizing the prey, baiting the trap, stalking the prey, springing the trap, and enjoying the wilderness."

Christine tried hard not to smile. Those were also good chapter titles for the book she had in mind. They could begin the book with pictures of eligible males and their vital statistics, followed by a chapter on how a woman could fix herself up to appeal to the victim of the hunt. Stalking the prey was similar to hunting down a man. How to get a man to propose certainly fit the "springing the trap" title. And "enjoying the wilderness" was certainly synonymous with planning a honeymoon.

"I think we should make the book as realistic as possible," Janelle said after a few moments of thought. "Live what we're writing about."

Peals of laughter bubbled from Christine. "I couldn't agree more. We'll make this a real hunter's guide!" *Now all I have to do is convince my dear sister her premise is great for a best seller, with just a twist in content!*

"You mean you're willing to spend the summer up at the cabin? You hate it there."

"I'll sacrifice."

Janelle eyed her sister suspiciously. "Something tells me I'm like the *Titanic*. I've hit the tip of the iceberg and I'm about to sink."

Laughing again, Christine patted Janelle's shoulder affectionately. "Trust me, twin. Just trust me."

"Now I know I'm in trouble. The last time—"

"No more fond memories. I've reformed! We'll spend this summer in the wholesome out-of-doors, tracking down game, scribbling notes on scraps of paper. And we'll make a fortune," she added gleefully.

Grabbing the footpost, Christine swung to her feet. Somehow, some way, she had to get some extremely attractive, eligible men up to the cabin. But how? She couldn't test any ideas if they were isolated in the wilderness by themselves. And Janelle would skin her alive and smoke her bones if she found out what she had planned. Never feeling thwarted by a challenge, she literally skipped out of her sister's bedroom.

She'd find a way, she assured herself. If necessity was the mother of invention, Christine Mc Mahon was a close relative. It was simply a matter of being creative. And sneaky!

David Mc Mahon thoughtfully returned the phone receiver to its cradle. Billy was in big trouble, he mused. The kind of trouble that can make a rock star burn himself out—woman trouble. Raking his hand over his furrowed brow he wondered if he'd given the Kid the right solution to his problem: get out, get away, get lost.

Who would have predicted Billy Carlton's affluent fans would have tracked him to an isolated island in the Bahamas? But this time they wouldn't find him. David had provided him with the perfect hideout: the family cabin in the Rockies. Silently David laughed to himself. Who would hunt for pop singer Billy Carlton, alias Billy the Kid, stuck away in the Colorado mountains? Everyone would look for him in Malibu, or Vegas, or maybe even in the hot spots of New York City, but never would the media expect the star to so isolate himself.

For once David Mc Mahon didn't have to worry about contacting his younger, scatterbrained sisters. They hadn't used the cabin in years. Undoubtedly Christine had another get-rich-quick scheme planned for their summer vacation.

"Thank goodness I'm two thousand miles away so they can't get me involved," he muttered as he remembered being scolded and chastised by their parents for being the ringleader. "Good ole Christine."

A smile curved his lips upward, changing his normally cynical expression. Christine couldn't help being an instigator. Perhaps genetically, weird chromosomes had been passed down from a skeleton in the family closet. The remainder of the family appeared staid, normal . . . sane, but then there was Christine.

Once as a youngster he remembered confiding a dream to be a young version of Evel Knievel, riding his bicycle at daring speeds, jumping over huge chasms. Courtesy of Christine, he found himself performing for the neighborhood children. Christine collected their quarters; he collected three broken bones in his hand and a broken wrist. And a stern lecture from their parents about being the oldest, the leader. He had to admit, however, that Christine had jumped to his defense and taken the blame. But no one believed such a sweet, innocent face could concoct anything even vaguely mischievous.

Maybe he should contact Janelle, just to make certain they weren't headed for the mountains. Then again, if he let Christine in on the scoop about the location of Billy the Kid, she'd probably start lining up local musicians for auditions and set up a concert outside the cabin. If anyone in the family should have been a talent agent, it should have been Christine. David chuckled aloud. No, he swiftly decided, he'd let sleeping dogs lie. Within days she could destroy what had taken him years to build.

Besides, Billy never traveled alone, and Big Nick could certainly handle any type of threat. Mentally David pictured Big Nick opposing his well-rounded sister, and he'd bet on Christine to win. Big Nick didn't stand a chance.

David picked up the telephone and dialed his twin sisters' residence.

"Christine? How's Colorado's favorite private entrepreneur?" he teased when he heard her voice.

"David!" Christine squealed. "Janelle and I were thinking about you earlier."

"I know. Don't tell me. You've decided to sell my bones to the medical center and you want me to sign a release form, right?"

"That's awful," Christine groaned. "Would I do something that morbid?"

Laughing, David replied, "Don't tell me you've grown scruples. What about the time you hid me under the bed, draped my arm, cut the hole in the jeweler's box, stuck my finger through it, powdered it, and tried to convince the neighborhood I'd been kidnapped and ransomed, and that you'd let them see the remains of my pinkie for fifty cents?"

"Kid stuff. I'm out of dimes and quarters and headed toward the big bucks."

"I'll sign the hospital release form. Promise to have them wait until I've met my demise, which I'm certain you're planning right now."

"David," she said, her voice full of reproach, "I love you. You're my darling brother."

"Uh-oh. Now I'm really worried. What little scheme are you cooking up?"

"I'm innocent." *Well, nearly innocent,* Christine amended to herself as she crossed her fingers. "Janelle and I are going to spend the summer writing a book which we're going to let you represent." She listened to his low groan of agony. "Now, don't groan again, David, until you've heard my idea. At first I thought about writing a romance, but everybody is doing that. So I altered the idea. What about a spoof on trapping a man?"

"It's been done before," David blurted out before considering the idea. "But wait a minute." Doing some quick mental gymnastics, he realized that if Christine and Janelle were busy writing a book, he wouldn't have to worry about Billy and Nick. "You're creative. Maybe you could think up some new twists," he enthused mildly. "Why don't you write up a synopsis and send it to me? I'll look it over and see if it's—"

"Oh, thanks, David! I knew we could count on you. This book will make us all millionaires!"

"Now, hold on, Sis. I'm not promising you the number-one slot on the *New York Times* best seller list. I'm not even promising I'll be able to sell it."

"You can!" Christine protested. "You represent some of the finest talent in America."

"Skip the sales pitch, Christine. I said I'd do it." David grinned at the simple solution to what could have been a hairy problem. "Get something in the mail to me in a couple of weeks, okay?"

"We'll start writing it immediately. David, you're such a wonderful brother. What would Janelle and I do without you?"

"I don't know, but there are times I'd like to find out," David quipped. "Something tells me you've already taken ten or fifteen years off my life-span."

"Why, David," Christine said, trying to sound hurt, "you don't mean that."

"I can almost see those sweet pouting lips hiding a wicked grin. You haven't changed, Christine, but someday you'll meet your match. However, I might add, I know I'm not it. While you're researching this piece of fluff, why don't you find a man who can match wits with you?"

"You're beginning to harp on that subject again. When I meet the right man I'll know it . . . and so will he."

"And if he doesn't; you'll convince him, hmm?"

"That's right, big brother," she agreed with a laugh. "I'd let you talk to Janelle, but she's at the store."

The last thing Christine wanted was for David to reveal the real topic of their book to Janelle. "When are you coming to visit your old hometown?" she asked, switching the subject abruptly.

"I'll be in Los Angeles later this summer, and I'm planning a brief stopover in Denver for a couple of days. Will you have the manuscript near completion?"

"Unless something unexpected happens."

David smiled at his sister's optimism. "Baby doll, with you the unexpected can be planned on."

"Don't give me that 'baby doll' baloney. You may foist your highfalutin big-city airs onto your other clients, but I know where all the skeletons are hidden in your family closet."

"Sorry. Baby doll is a protective device that has become a habit. You haven't any idea how many phone calls I get from women who expect me to recognize their voices."

"Poor mistreated brother. Maybe I should come to New York—"

"The other phone is ringing. See you later this summer . . . in Denver!" David concluded with a laugh. "Give my love to Janelle."

"Love you too, David. Bye."

Christine resisted the urge to rub her hands together with excitement. In a moment of fantasy she pictured the three Mc Mahons being interviewed by the press. She and Janelle were dripping ermine and diamonds as they smiled at the reporters. David, suave, a dark-haired version of Janelle, would introduce them to the rich, the famous. Christine clamped her fingers over her mouth to stifle a giggle.

CHAPTER TWO

"The first thing we'll do when we get there is unpack the groceries, then get the bedrooms halfway respectable," Janelle explained as they turned off the highway onto the winding wilderness road. Christine, tired from the hectic pace of getting the students out of the building for the summer, wanted to collapse and sleep for at least a week.

Tall aspen, pine, and spruce trees changed twilight into darkness. With the headlights on, Janelle concentrated on following the ill-kept road at a snail's pace.

"I'd forgotten how deserted it is up here," Christine muttered, bracing her arms on the Jeep's dashboard. "Civilization's uncharted territory. Didn't David pay Zeke to take care of the road and the house? What if the house is in as poor condition as the road?"

"Then we'll fix it up ourselves. Thanks to our remodeling job last summer, there isn't much I can't fix," Janelle replied.

"How much further?" Christine used her favorite traveling ploy to change the subject.

Janelle laughed. "Ah, that's your favorite question every time we travel. You're worse than a ten-year-old."

"Too bad we don't have a magic carpet. Anything has to be smoother than this skeleton-crunching vehicle."

"You're the one who wanted to trade in our old Chevy," Janelle reminded her, then chuckled. "You just didn't expect me to buy a four-wheel-drive Jeep."

"You said a *racy* sports car. I pictured one of those cute little Mustangs."

"Now you see why I bought the Jeep. Incidentally, we have less than twenty miles to go. You want to drive the last stretch?"

"Very funny. You know darn well that every time we get on the side of this mountain I feel as though I'm about to fall off." Christine glanced at her twin and couldn't tell whether Janelle nodded or the last swimming-pool-size pothole made her head bounce up and down. "Haven't you ever noticed that Zeke's left leg is longer than his right leg? Comes from standing on the side of the mountain too long," she explained as her lower jaw slammed shut on the tip of her tongue.

Christine decided to keep her mouth closed rather than risk going through life with a permanent lisp. Silently she cursed each bump, Mother Nature, and her sister for bringing her deeper and deeper into the wilderness. There wasn't any doubt in her mind as to what they would find when they pulled up in front of the family cabin: the ramshackle place would be a mess. No telling what would be on the inside.

She rubbed the tip of her tongue against the back of her teeth to make certain it hadn't become a casualty of the road. Sore, but there, she thought. Little did the reading public know the agonies she was going through to provide them with a best seller.

"One more hairpin curve and we'll be there," Janelle commented enthusiastically. Rounding the curve she saw a beam of light. "Ah-ha! See? Zeke did know we were coming. There's a light on in the living room."

"At least he kept the generator working. We won't have to go without luxuries like hot water, a stove, and lights to read by. God knows there isn't much else to enjoy up here," Christine griped.

Slowly braking the car in front of the cabin, Janelle grinned at the expected complaints. "I could drive you back and spend the summer up here by myself," she suggested, knowing full well the response she'd get.

"No way," Christine answered firmly. "We're here on business. While you're out stalking the prey, I'm going to be scribbling in the spiral notebooks I brought along. By the end of the summer the manuscript will be finished and we'll be rich and famous."

"Zeke didn't keep up the road, but the house looks great from what I can see," Janelle said as she opened the door. "Bring in a sack of groceries, will you? I'll carry in the luggage."

Christine climbed out of what she considered a torture chamber and slowly straightened as a wealth of happy childhood memories flooded over her. She could almost hear her dad shouting at the top of his lungs, banging the iron bell on the front porch, calling the three of them out of the woods to come in for a meal. The memory of the best lemon meringue pie west of the Mississippi and homemade corn bread sharpened her taste buds.

How many times had they carefully constructed a circle of rocks and roasted marshmallows as they spun ghostly stories of haunted mine shafts and marauding Indians? Funny, she thought, smiling, it was only the good times she remembered. She wondered if the reason she disliked the idea of returning to the family mountain retreat was partially due to nothing being the same. David was in New York; she and Janelle were teaching in Denver; their parents were gone. Bottled in her memory, the good times threatened to spill forth in the form of tears.

Janelle slid the suitcase on the wooden porch, turned, and took a deep breath. "It's good to be back, isn't it?"

Choking back her tears, Christine answered as she walked to the steps and hugged her sister around the waist, "I can almost smell the corn bread baking. You don't think that sweet old hermit, Zeke, has dinner waiting for us, do you?"

Sniffing, Janelle cocked her head to one side

toward the door. "I smell it too. Let's play Goldilocks and investigate."

Before they had taken another step, the screen door creaked open. Christine could feel her eyes rounding when she saw a man as big as a grizzly bear and just about as furry close the door behind himself.

"Who?" she squeaked. "What?"

Both of them stumbled backward in surprise. Off-balance, her arms flailing wildly to steady herself, Christine unceremoniously plunked down hard on her backside. She heard muffled laughter, but from the corner of her eye she didn't see the big man even smile.

"Look what you did!" Janelle accused, rushing to her twin's side. "Get the hell off my property!"

"Ma'am," the giant drawled in a soft Southern accent, "you're trespassing. Now, why don't you two little ladies mosey on back to wherever you came from. Otherwise I'll have to call the local sheriff."

"You great lummox, you don't have a phone!" Janelle retorted. "Why don't you go get the sheriff? We'll see who's trespassing."

Christine rose unsteadily to her feet and dusted the back of her faded blue jeans off with both hands. "I'm okay," she mumbled, knowing Janelle protectively hovered between herself and man mountain. "Who the hell are you?" she quizzed once her head had cleared.

"Doesn't matter who I am. I don't hold to

gettin' rough with ladies, but . . ." Slowly he advanced to the edge of the porch.

Protective instincts overruling sound judgment, Janelle hurled herself against the threatening male. "Run, Christine! Run! I'll hold him off."

Christine heard Janelle's foot whack into the giant's shin, but temporarily she couldn't move. Janelle wasn't any match for the huge man. She couldn't run off and leave her sister at his mercy. She ran up the steps and clamped her teeth on the log-size arm reaching out for her sister.

"Ooooouch!" the assailant bellowed, seemingly confused by the double onslaught. "Billllllyyy!"

Oh, my God, there's another one, Christine thought, biting down harder. Her eyes darted to the darkened screen door.

Janelle had both hands in the giant's long dark hair and was shaking his head back and forth. Feet dangling, she kicked as hard as she could.

"Damned hellcattin' groupies," Christine heard between male grunts. The man defended himself, trying to block Janelle's blows and dislodge her teeth from his arm, but he didn't seem to be fighting back.

He was probably some loner type like Zeke who thought he'd found a good cabin to summer in, Christine surmised, shaking her head, ripping the sleeve of the brute's shirt. Again she heard what she could have sworn was muffled laughter.

"Let them go." The softly spoken command cut through the grunts and groans.

"Let go? Hell! They're the ones chewin' my arm off and rippin' my beard out," the giant panted. "Make *them* let loose!"

Christine heard the screen door creak, then felt the strong arms of a determined man latch around her waist and gently but firmly tug her loose. Once her teeth had been removed from the big man's shirt, she felt herself twirled around and imprisoned, wrists behind her back, against the length of a strange man.

"Help! Zeke! Help!" Christine knew Zeke couldn't hear her shout, but she also knew the strangers wouldn't know that fact.

"Zeke? The old-timer?" the stranger crooned against her ear. "He's the one who prepared the cabin for us."

"Like hell!" Christine refuted. Panting, she squirmed to free her hands but couldn't budge beneath his iron grip.

"Calm down," he soothed. "There's been some sort of mix-up. Calm down."

Looking up, Christine could only see fair hair and sunglasses. Sunglasses? In the dark? What was he? A druggie? An outlaw?

She forced herself to relax. Struggling only brought her closer into his arms. Much closer and she wouldn't be able to breathe, she thought, shutting her eyes.

"That's better. Nick? You okay?" His voice never rose above a pleasant level.

"I've got mine subdued . . ." The grunt he gave told everyone Janelle had lambasted him again.

"Let's all sit down, calmly, and find out what the problem is," the man holding Christine suggested. "A friend loaned us the cabin for a month or so."

Lowering herself into a cane-backed chair, Christine scoffed, "That's impossible. We own the cabin."

"What's your name?"

"What's *your* name?" Christine drilled. "You're the trespasser. You should be the one answering the questions."

She watched a secretive glance pass between the blond with the sunglasses and the huge dark-haired man. Obviously her captor was the boss. If she hadn't been watching carefully, she wouldn't have seen the dark-haired man shake his head from side to side.

"David Mc Mahon—"

"That's a lie," Christine interrupted. "I know David Mc Mahon when I see him."

"Now we're getting somewhere. David Mc Mahon loaned us the cabin." The blond man leaned against the railing around the porch. "Does he represent you?"

A nervous giggle bubbled from between Christine's lips. "He's our brother."

The swing Janelle sat on groaned a protest as she hopped to her feet. "Christine talked to

David in New York. He knew we were coming up here for the summer." With her blue eyes still blazing, she turned to Christine. "Didn't he?"

All heads swung in Christine's direction. She shrugged nonchalantly in an effort to appear innocent. "Would you take off your sunglasses? It's disconcerting to have a conversation with a person when you can't see his eyes."

She almost sighed with relief when everyone's eyes shifted away from her. She realized she hadn't told David exactly where they would be writing the book, but at the time it seemed unimportant. He should have told her he planned on loaning out the cabin.

The night sounds of the forest could be heard in the lull in conversation. The still unidentified blond stranger slowly raised his hand. He fingered the wire frames of his reflective sunglasses, then he bent his head and removed them.

Christine and Janelle both audibly gasped. He had the darkest, most beautiful eyes either of them had ever seen. Although the beam of light from the curtained window was minimal, it all appeared to be clustered in the depths of his eyes.

"They recognize you," the huge man grumbled. "We'll never get rid of them."

"Are you crooks?" Christine blurted out. "My brother the agent is representing criminals?" Her voice rose an octave at the incredible idea. None of the pieces of the puzzle fit together. "Just who the devil are you?"

"Wait a minute, Christine. I know who he is. Aren't you . . . ?"

"Yeah! We've got a couple of his albums. You practically swoon when you—"

"Shut up, Christine," Janelle warned in a decidedly sweet voice. "Billy Carlton? Billy the Kid!"

"Guilty as charged," Billy replied, obviously not pleased that he had been recognized. "He's Big Nick, my bodyguard." The last two words were coated with restrained laughter.

"So much for peace and quiet," Nick commented. "The minute they leave, every newspaper in Colorado will know your whereabouts."

Christine watched the light fade out of the pop singer's eyes. She could feel the disappointment in the mountain air. Clearing her throat she rose to her full height, all five feet two. "Well, since you don't want to be discovered here, I guess you'll have to leave. We certainly don't want groupies tearing up our property to get to you."

"Try paying them off," Big Nick suggested to Billy. "David wouldn't take money, but maybe they will."

The short dark hairs on Christine's neck bristled. *First he called us groupies, now he's insinuating we're gold diggers!* She glared at the huge hulk of a man. Choosing the least reputable of the two, she fulfilled his expectations by asking, "How much?"

"Hold on, Christine. We can't charge David's clients," Janelle protested, taking a step toward Billy. "David must have misunderstood about us using the cabin for the summer."

Christine watched her twin's lips curve into a generous smile as she looked at the singer. Had Janelle been starstruck? Her imagination cranked up to full speed ahead. Janelle and Billy made a perfect pair. Wouldn't it be romantic if Billy fell head over heels for Janelle? He had everything: wealth, good looks, fame. What more could she want for her sister?

"How does ten thousand sound? Four nice round zeros behind a one," Christine suggested, harboring a delightful smile behind her hand. She named the outrageous price to make Billy think they were interested in his money. Women pursued him. Let him think they weren't interested in him personally.

Those darker than brown, almost black eyes of Billy Carlton raked over her from the crown of her head, over her curvaceous figure, to the tips of her strappy sandals. "I wonder if you'd take the money," he mused aloud.

"We aren't taking his money," Janelle ground out between clenched teeth. It was one thing for Christine to earn money through wild schemes, but this little idea stank. "Come on, sister dear, we're going home."

"I'm not going back over those roads at

night." She pointed in Big Nick's direction. "Let them pay up or leave."

"Why does anyone have to leave?" Billy questioned. "The cabin is big enough to accommodate all of us."

Christine nearly crowed with delight. *Don't capitulate too easily*, she warned herself. Making her expression appear skeptical of the idea, she asked, "Just because we stay, does that mean you don't pay?"

Billy quietly restrained Janelle from grabbing Christine's arm by taking a step in between them. "I'll pay."

His eyes searched through the darkness into Christine's. He saw the contained mirth. Lightly he placed his hands on her upper arms. He wanted to feel her soft skin beneath his fingertips. Professionally he had dealt with a multitude of would-be starlets and publicity seekers, as well as money-hungry women. Christine wasn't any one of the three. Her brown eyes held golden elements of secretiveness, but they weren't shrewd or conniving.

"Why don't we sit down over dinner and finalize an agreement?" he suggested in a low, sultry voice.

The wedding march hummed in Christine's ears. As maid of honor she'd have the perfect view of her twin being wed to this tall, awe-inspiring celebrity. She could hear them begging her to accompany them on a world cruise, but of course she would turn down their generous offer. They'd have beautiful blond babies, one with dark eyes, one with blue, and she, the children's favorite aunt, would be invited to their mansion in . . .

Janelle moved to her side and pinched her arm before Christine could get to the grandchildren. "What are you up to? You know perfectly well David would strangle you if you took one red cent from them," she whispered.

"Isn't he dreamy?" Christine responded, wanting to know if her sister was attracted to Billy.

"Dreamy," Janelle confirmed, but refusing to be sidetracked, she hissed, "Not one penny, you hear me?"

"Do you still like to dance?"

"Christine Mc Mahon," she whispered, exasperated, "what does dancing have to do with your bilking Mr. Carlton out of money?"

"He's a good dancer. You've seen his musical videos. I just thought . . ."

"Have you ladies finished the family conference? We're eating dinner in the kitchen if you don't mind." Big Nick held his arms out, directing them to the kitchen as though it weren't their house. "Beans and ham and corn bread."

Christine led the way to the table. Four places were set. With his sunglasses back in place, Billy held a chair out for her as Nick seated Janelle across the table. As the men sat down in the end chairs, Christine wondered why Billy found it necessary to wear sunglasses inside the house. Did normal lighting cause him discomfort? It was undoubtedly a Hollywood affectation, she decided. Nick had brought four plates heaped with generous helpings of beans and ham.

"Butter?" Nick asked, passing the dish to Christine. He glanced from Billy to both women as though he'd been chosen as the spokesman for the two men. "We both came here planning to stay in the same cabin. Correct?"

Christine nodded. She took a pat of butter and spread it over the corn bread. She kept a close watch on Billy. *Why,* she wondered, *is the man in charge delegating his authority to his bodyguard? Shouldn't he be the one speaking?* It was his money; he should have been the one negotiating.

The impulse to reach to her right and pluck the glasses off his nose made her fingers itch. How was she supposed to have any inkling of what was going on in his mind when he had silver-toned mirrors perched on his nose?

"My sister and I have important work to do here that we can't accomplish in Denver." She reached under the table and nudged her twin's foot to keep her silent.

Nick forked a man-size bite of beans into his mouth and chewed thoughtfully. After swallowing, he looked to Billy for his cue and pointed his fork in Janelle's direction. "What kind of important work?"

"We're writing a book about women hunters," Janelle answered succinctly.

The glasses moving from side to side was the only overt indication that Billy was directly perusing each of them. "Authors?"

"Aspiring writers," Janelle replied.

Nick interpreted. "Unpublished scribblers," he said, grinning.

Like a kitten whose fur had been stroked backward, Christine bristled. "Not all of us were raised with a platinum microphone in our mouths."

If memory served her right, Billy was the only child of the famous Carltons. Throughout his childhood and teenage years his parents had groomed him for stardom. And in the past five years he had gained independent fame.

Although she saw a thinning of the pop singer's lips, it was Nick who visibly reacted. His bushy black brows winged upward then swooped lower than normal as his blue eyes impaled her with a dangerous stare. "But you don't mind using your brother to guarantee getting published, do you?"

Christine had the grace to blush at his accurate assessment of her exact intentions. "That's different."

She glanced at Billy and saw him make a slight, quick cutting motion with his forefinger. He smiled benignly as though her jab hadn't pricked his thick hide.

"Back to the main problem. Billy is willing to reimburse you for the use of"—he paused significantly—"the cabin. He's also willing to allow you to stay here as long as you don't interfere with his work."

"Diplomacy," Billy muttered.

The single word of chastisement had an immediate effect on Big Nick.

Lowering his voice back to its Southern drawl, Nick added, "We'd appreciate your cooperation. Finding isolated lodging is difficult."

Christine's head swiveled between the two men. Billy evidently wasn't about to allow his lackey to antagonize her, even though Nick's size and his tense, ready-to-defend-his-boss attitude was enough to intimidate almost anyone. But what he didn't realize was that Christine had been sheltered by Janelle in much the same manner. Regardless of the outrageous situations she had managed to get them into, Janelle backed her to the hilt. And right now Christine could feel the supportive pressure of Janelle's foot against her own.

Inwardly Christine giggled. How was Big Nick going to compete with Janelle's protective instincts once Billy and Janelle were married? He'd probably find himself on the unemployment line. Mentally she pictured the hairy hulk towering over the supervisor at the office, demanding somebody to guard. Maybe, after David sold their book for thousands of dollars, she'd hire him. Christine grinned. She loved a solid dose of poetic justice.

"Ms. Mc Mahon? Are you woolgathering or making a decision?" Nick asked.

Flashing Billy a cheeky grin, she quipped,

"Since we're going to be living together, I guess we can dispense with the formalities. I'm Christine Mc Mahon, and the beautiful lady across the table from me is my twin, Janelle."

Christine kept the perky smile in place even though her twin lightly mashed her toe to remind Christine that she hated being introduced as the beauty of the family.

"Elizabeth Taylor," she heard Billy murmur, his head turned in her direction.

"Pardon?" Christine questioned.

"You remind him of Elizabeth Taylor," Nick explained when Billy continued eating.

Self-consciously Christine shook her head. "During her fat years?"

"No," Billy said softly.

Unaccustomed to flattery of any sort, Christine felt flustered by his scrutiny. *The poor fellow must have on rose-colored distorted glasses to make such a drastic mistake!* "Janelle is the beautiful twin."

Janelle, her face bright red, kicked her sister's shin. "You'll have to excuse Christine. As a child she read too many fairy tales where one sister was beautiful and the other wicked."

Everyone laughed but Christine.

"And to set the record straight," Janelle continued, "we won't accept any money for your staying here. You're our brother's guests. Had we known you were here we would have stayed in Denver. In fact, we can go back—"

"Oh, no, we won't," Christine barged in. "They can stay, but so do we!"

Raising his glasses and propping them on his head, Billy focused his eyes on Christine. "We wouldn't dream of interfering with your creative endeavors. Do you prefer the top floor or the bottom floor?" He smiled somewhat wistfully and added, "I suppose coeducational mixing of the bedrooms is out of the question."

His black eyes and the half smile seemed to grab Christine's heart and vigorously shake it. For a fleeting moment she wondered what sharing a bedroom with Billy Carlton would be like. The warmth emanating from his eyes heated her blood, making her face burn—and her fingertips tingle.

"Hollywood stars aren't bright enough to thaw a Colorado mountain girl," she replied in her coolest voice as she tried to hide her flustered state.

The moment he lowered his glasses back into place, Christine wished she had bitten off the tip of her tongue earlier in the car. His face assumed a passive mask, but she could feel his hurt as though it were tangible.

"Okay, sweetheart," Nick drawled, rubbing his arm that had a semicircle of red marks caused by her teeth, "withdraw your fangs. We've put our gear upstairs. Any objections?"

"None," Janelle replied. "Christine can take David's room, and I'll take our parents' room."

Unable to curb her curiosity, Christine leaned toward Billy. "Which room are you in upstairs?"

"Yours."

CHAPTER THREE

How does he know it's my bedroom? Christine wondered.

"The unicorns," Billy answered as though he had heard her question. Her eyes seemed to probe behind his glasses, but he couldn't let her through the protective wall they provided. From the things he'd learned about her by living in her room, he was tempted to trust her, to let her get close to him. But he'd been wrong before, and repeatedly hurt. No, he mused, it was wiser, safer, to keep the reflective barrier between them until she earned his trust.

"The posters on the walls?" she quizzed. *Damn the man.* Every time he plopped his California shades on his nose they affected his tongue. Couldn't he string together more than two-word answers when his pupils were covered? Why didn't he take them off?

"Yeah," Nick answered. "I took the room with the oversize animal photographs. Must belong to you, huh?" he asked, directing his question to Janelle.

Janelle nodded, then teased, "I'll bet you felt right at home, didn't you."

Laughing good-naturedly, Nick picked up his empty dishes and headed toward the sink. "I haven't dealt with any wild animals that could compete with you. Am I missing hunks of my beard?"

When Christine saw Janelle getting up, she jumped to her feet. "Big Nick and I will clean up," she volunteered. "Why don't you take Billy down to the creek?"

Alone on a moonlight stroll they wouldn't be able to resist each other, Christine mused, grinning at the thought of Janelle returning a bit mussed up, eyes glowing from discovering her attraction to Billy.

"My chore," Billy stated decisively.

"Oh, no," Christine protested, realizing she'd be alone with him, and Janelle would be with Big Nick.

"Can you walk through the forest quietly?" Janelle asked Nick. "There should be animals feeding near the creek."

Christine felt her manipulations slipping through her fingers. "I'll take him to the creek. You stay here and do the dishes."

"No way, sister dear. You'd shoot Nick and claim you thought he was a grizzly. I'm the outdoors woman, remember?"

"But . . ." Although her mind was whirling, Christine couldn't find a logical, convincing reason to negate the plan.

"You wash and I'll dry," Billy suggested. A

knowing smile curved his lips upward. He dismissed Nick with a sharp nod of his head.

Billy had watched Christine throughout dinner, trying to figure out exactly what she was up to. Years of being in the limelight made him acutely aware of women who flirted, then arranged for a secluded twosome. Christine was still sputtering as Nick and her sister departed. She wasn't the least intrigued by him. In fact, she had been willing to show Nick around the property rather than help him with the dishes. Why? he wondered.

The bottle of dishwashing detergent clutched in her hand, Christine wished it was her sister's throat as she squeezed it. *Obtuse woman!* Didn't Janelle realize the big game trophy was right here in the kitchen? Minus the sunglasses, they made a beautiful matched set. Both blond, both tall and slender, both somewhat reserved, they were made for each other.

"Angry?" Billy asked as he swept crumbs off the table into his hand.

Thwarted, she fumed silently, turning the faucet on full blast. A rush of water hit the soap, forming suds instantaneously and splashing them out of the sink. She jumped back just as Billy reached around her to turn the faucet down.

"Oh! Sorry," she exclaimed immediately, stepping away from any physical contact with him.

Chuckling at her inviting pursed mouth and

the brief collision of her rounded bottom against his thighs, he gently swiped a frothy blob of suds off the tip of her nose.

"Don't be," he said. "My pleasure."

Christine saw twin images of herself reflected in his aviator glasses. The mirrored image made her dark eyes appear huge, her nose small, her chin nonexistent. *Remove the damned glasses*, she mentally blasted.

When he did remove them and tuck them in his shirt pocket, Christine once again felt the full effect of his mesmerizing dark eyes. Confused by the devastating effect they had on her nervous system, she quickly turned back to the sink and shut the faucet off.

"Why don't you fix some coffee while I start the dishes?" she suggested, aware of his remaining within easy touching distance. "Janelle will be cold by the time they return."

His fingers, curled, scant inches from her shoulders, relaxed as he lowered them back to his sides. What was the undeniable attraction? Why did he have the urge to cuddle her in his arms, taste her lips? He backed away and followed her suggestion.

Begin the campaign, Christine ordered herself. "Isn't Janelle lovely?" she asked.

Billy had one woman on his mind and it wasn't her sister. "Lovely," he replied, covertly watching her small hands diving into the suds, wishing they were serving the more pleasurable purpose of stroking his chest instead of performing such a mundane task.

The smile she cast over her shoulder beguiled him further.

Now we're getting somewhere, she mused triumphantly. "She's always been unassuming about her beauty. Everyone admires her."

Allowing himself the pleasure of an unrestricted view of her, he abstractly answered, "Um-hmm."

She would challenge him to live up to her high ideals. A man who had everything money could buy, and thousands of screaming women begging for his favors, couldn't resist the unobtainable.

"And she's a fine teacher. Loves children. I think secretly she'd like to start a family of her own if she met someone who measures up to her high standards."

"All the Mc Mahons have high standards," Billy responded, more interested in the way her snug jeans cupped her rear end than continuing the conversation.

Short but delightfully put together, he concluded, silently laughing at her self-image of being fat. Her soft curves appealed to him. He had managed to measure scoops of ground coffee into the filter of the automatic coffee maker without his thoughts causing a spill. He picked up the plastic measuring container and moved to the sink to fill it with water.

Christine scooted to the left. She was aware of his exact location without seeing or hearing him. A thick lump settled in the back of her throat and refused to dissolve. Her head tilted upward as she watched him move the spigot to the other side of the double stainless steel sink and begin to fill the container with cold water.

Her dark eyes flowed over his strong masculine profile. Broad forehead, straight short nose, a thin upper lip matched with a fuller, sensuous lower lip, his jaw set as though his teeth were clamped together, a stubble of evening growth spread over his cheeks until it reached the hollows beneath his prominent cheekbones, each individual feature had her fingers tingling beneath the soapsuds. The plate she ineffectually washed clanked to the bottom of the sink.

Billy turned off the faucet and set the plastic container on the drainboard. He edged closer until he barely touched the side of her foot, thigh, and hips. Pretending to be fascinated by the suds on the water, he cupped his hand and scooped the foam upward like a small cumulus cloud caught in the forces of nature.

"I should have offered to wash the dishes," he stated, letting the suds slip through his fingers. His cupped fingers skirted the edges of the sink for another handful.

Christine inched further to the left. Each place the fabric of their clothing touched seemed warmer than those untouched. Uncomfortable with the strange sensation, uncomfortable with the wild thoughts spinning haphazardly through her mind about her future brother-in-law, she withdrew one hand

and braced herself on the flat Formica counter top.

Billy couldn't remember ever doing dishes. Chuckling, he shared the thought with her. "Believe it or not, I've never done dishes."

"You're kidding," she said in what she hoped was a level tone. Forcing humor into her voice, she grinned and joked, "Mr. Hollywood experiences a Rocky Mountain high . . . dishpan hands."

Billy looped his thumb and forefinger around her small wrist and raised her clenched hand. Suds clung to the knuckles and the pad of flesh beneath her cocked thumb.

"Open up," he ordered. Using his dry hand he gently uncurled her fingers. With one finger he hopscotched over the lines of her palm. "Aren't your fingertips supposed to look like shriveled prunes?" he questioned. His eyes moved from the palm of her hand to her face while his thumb pressed against her love line.

Resisting the urge to clench her fingers around his thumb, she refused to look into his questioning eyes. Christine numbly shook her head.

"Yours are pink." He raised her hand upward for closer inspection.

The water dribbling over her wrist and down her arm gave her the excuse she needed to pull away. Hastily she wiped her hands on the cotton dish towel hanging over the sink. She had to say something to explain herself, but her mouth was dry. Her tongue stuck to the roof of her mouth.

Where's your wit? For heaven's sake, think of something funny to say.

"You wash and I'll dry. I wouldn't want you to be deprived of one of life's little pleasures," she babbled, uncertain the words passed through her lips distinctly enough to be understood. To her own ears they sounded slurred.

Billy grinned as he watched her hasty departure. He wondered if she felt the same attraction he felt from the moment he grabbed her on the porch. The grin spread wider as he watched her pour the water into the drip coffee maker. Her lips moved slightly as though she were talking to herself.

"What's taking Janelle and Nick so long?" she muttered, wanting to revive her initial purpose in conversing with Billy Carlton.

He flashed her a wicked grin and began humming the old standard, "Makin' Whoopie."

"Change deprived to depraved, Mr. Carlton. My sister doesn't make whoopie with strangers," she said, staunchly defending Janelle.

"What about her twin?" he boldly teased. "I may not be experienced at doing household chores, but . . ." He wiggled his hips in a manner that nearly incited riots at his concerts.

Impulsively Christine twisted the dish towel between her hands and popped him on the rear end with the tip.

"What about her twin?" he repeated.

Christine twisted the truth with the same ease with which she had twisted the towel. "Twins think alike. I wouldn't consider—"

"You aren't a carbon copy of your sister in appearance," he interrupted. "Does her behavior regulate yours?"

"Of course not, Mr. Carlton," she said formally. "Janelle and I don't look alike, and to be truthful—"

"I've never washed dishes and you've never made whoopie in the kitchen."

"Stop interrupting me!"

"I beg your pardon," he responded in a most unapologetic tone. His tongue rolled in his cheek as he glanced over his shoulder and slowly lowered one eyelid.

The slow, sexy wink made her want to wring her hands to keep them from tracing the path his tongue made in the hollow of his cheek. *Keep your hands to yourself. Keep them busy*, she warned. She reached for the pan of corn bread on the table.

"Where was I before I was so rudely interrupted?" she asked. Her eyes bounced from the aluminum pan to the laughter she saw lighting his devilish eyes.

"You were about to be truthful. Please continue."

The pan clattered to the floor. Christine cursed her clumsiness. Any pretense of denying the desire to make whoopie with the handsome pop singer was forgotten when she peered over the table and saw the mess she had made. The low, throaty chuckle she heard didn't help restore her jangled nerves either.

"See what you made me do?"

Billy pulled his hands out of the water and began drying them on the dish towel. "I'll clean it up."

"No, you won't. House rule: Clean up your own mess and you won't get yelled at."

"Who's yelling?"

Their knees touched as Billy crouched down beside her. Christine flinched as if she'd received an electric shock. *He doesn't have to yell,* she silently admitted. With his sex appeal turned up to full volume, she knew she wouldn't be able to hear him if he did shout.

Her eyes lifted to the deep vee formed by the open collar of his pale sport shirt. Somehow or another he'd managed to get suds on his chest. As though they had a will of their own, her fingers flicked a cluster of bubbles away from the golden hairs on his chest.

"What the hell is going on here?" a voice boomed from the doorway. "Is she attacking you again?"

Christine and Billy sprang apart like two guilty children caught playing doctor. Sheepishly Christine glanced at her sister's stunned face.

"It's okay," Billy answered, laughing. "We're just"—he shrugged meaningfully—"cleaning up."

Her eyes glued to her toes, Christine noticed the hunks of corn bread still on the floor. Excusing herself, she scuttled over to the closet and pulled out the broom and dustpan.

"Here. I'll help with that," Billy offered, flashing Christine a devilish wink.

"You've helped enough," she muttered, chagrined by the speculative expression on Nick's face.

As she stooped to clean up the mess she cast an apologetic look toward her sister. She used more force than necessary to sweep the crumbs, and they flew over the dustpan instead of into it. A muted groan passed between her lips. "He started it," she mumbled, hoping Janelle and Nick would see her role in the accident a minor one.

Billy took the broom from her hand, threw back his head, and laughed boisterously. "We aren't going to be spanked for being naughty," he chortled. "It was good clean fun," he punned as he swept water and suds toward the dustpan.

Janelle groaned aloud. Christine moaned silently as she strained her neck upward and gave him a that-was-really-a-bad-one look.

"I should have known better than to leave you alone with her. She tried to amputate my arm," Nick said to Billy. He moved between Billy and Christine in bodyguard fashion. He peered down from his great height and looked at Christine. "Why don't you run along to bed? Janelle told me you were exhausted."

With most of the damage in the immediate area cleaned up, Christine stood up. She wished she could tower over both of the men the way they towered over her. "I'm a bit old to be sent to bed," she scoffed with a dignified sniff.

When she saw Billy's lopsided grin and his raised blond eyebrow, she clenched her hand. If he had been David, she would have given him a sly punch and scampered off to bed like an angelic, dutiful daughter. But instead she straightened her shoulders and marched toward the door. She could hear footsteps behind her. Prepared to smack Billy for having the audacity to follow her, she wheeled around.

"I'm tired too," Janelle said, noticing the fire in her sister's eyes. "Do you think we could get to sleep without a pillow fight?" she teased.

Christine gave Janelle a weak smile and turned toward the back bedrooms. "Maybe an exchange of sisterly confidences?"

"You were playing in there, weren't you? At first it looked like . . ." Janelle left the impression dangling between them.

"Of course." Christine walked into her sister's assigned room and plopped down in the wingback chair by the bed. She watched Janelle lift her suitcase off the floor, set it on the bed, and begin unpacking. "I guess my hand pressed against his chest did look a bit . . . peculiar."

"Good choice of words," Janelle replied. She tossed aside a nightgown and stowed a pile of lingerie in the top dresser drawer. "What do you think of Billy?" she inquired thoughtfully.

"He's not what a pop singer is supposed to be like," Christine hedged. She was caught between wanting to extoll his virtues and disclaiming any interest in him. "What do you think?"

"I can see why his fans wilt under those eyes. God made a mistake giving them to a man instead of a woman. His lashes must be at least an inch long."

Now we're getting somewhere, Christine mused. She'd focused the direction of the conversation on encouraging Janelle to openly admire him.

"But Nick is more my type," Janelle said, pulling a stack of shorts and tops out of the suitcase.

"No, he isn't," Christine blurted. Her plan disintegrated. "He's big and hairy. You're classy and sleek. The two of you make a classic 'Beauty and the Beast' tale in my estimation."

"You and your fairy tales," Janelle scoffed. "You've always thought a prince would come riding into my life on a white charger and carry me away to his castle."

"There's nothing wrong with the story line if you'd cooperate. Big Nick," she grumbled, shaking her head as she prepared to do a hatchet job on him, "is a bodyguard."

Janelle's blue eyes twinkled with amusement. "You'd better check the back covers on the stack of records I brought along. Billy introducing Big Nick as his bodyguard is an inside joke between the two of them."

"Don't tell me who he really is. Let me guess." Christine responded the way she used to when her twin masked her face in mystery. "He's Billy's long-lost brother."

"Nope. You only get three guesses," her twin replied. "Bedroom chores?" she queried, stipulating the penalty for whoever lost the guessing game.

With a gleam in her dark eyes, Christine nodded. "Nick is a disguised rock musician?"

"Nope. That's two. One more and you'll be making my bed and picking up my clothes tomorrow."

"Hmph!" Christine tapped her finger on her cheeks as she contemplated what capacity Nick played in the rock star's life. The only clue her sister had given was the back covers of the records. In some way he had to be connected with the music business, but she couldn't picture him as anything more than a stagehand moving heavy equipment around. And a roadie certainly didn't get recognition on an album cover.

"Ten seconds," Janelle warned, reminding her of the time limit in the game. "Nine, eight, seven, . . ."

"He's a photographer!" she guessed wildly. "He does the front covers."

"Wrong. Nick writes the lyrics for Billy's songs," Janelle bubbled enthusiastically.

"That mountain-size man writes songs?" Christine exclaimed, disbelief written clearly

57

on her face. "Boy, did he feed you a line of bull!"

"You're the English teacher. Ever read anything by Nicolas Gentry?"

"Gullible, gullible, gullible Janelle Mc Mahon. Nicolas Gentry and Big Nick aren't one and the same. He's stringing you along." Christine rose to her feet and walked to the door. "There's a string loose in your guitar if you believe that lie."

Grinning, Janelle bent over to finish emptying the suitcase. "I'd like my room clean before noon, please," she cooed triumphantly.

"Uh-huh. Sure. I'll have Big Nick the poet in here bright and early. You lose this one, sister dear. Next you'll be gullible enough to ask his advice on our book."

"I did ask, and he will help!" Janelle crowed. "With Nick as a coauthor we won't have any trouble getting David to market the book. He's already Nick's agent."

Christine had the sinking feeling she escaped from having dishpan hands, but scullery maid's knees and elbows were about to become her fate.

"I'm going to check it out first," she vowed. "Care to make the penalty for being gullible a two-week stint of maid service instead of one day?" she added, bluffing.

"Make it easy on yourself," Janelle answered glibly. "I'll leave a record cover on my unmade bed. Nick and I are going to go bird watching early in the morning."

Stymied by her twin's complete acceptance of the whopping lie Nick had spun, she shook her head with mock sadness and gently closed the bedroom door.

Nicolas Gentry, she silently scoffed as she crossed the hallway to the other bedroom. His beefy hand was too big to hold a pencil, much less write sensitive poetry. Famous poet or not, he wasn't suitable for her twin. Billy Carlton was. And she certainly didn't want Nick to get his big paws on the manuscript she planned to write with her sister. That would spell disaster in capital letters.

She glanced up toward the ceiling when she heard the bed overhead squeak.

He's going to belong to Janelle, she vowed. *They're perfect together.*

She changed into her nightgown and stretched out on the bed. In the darkness the sounds coming from overhead seemed louder. Much as she tried to bar her mind from thinking about the fun they'd had in the kitchen, she caught herself grinning from ear to ear.

When she heard single notes melodically being strung together into a soft lullabye, she covered her head with the blankets. *Think of him as your future brother-in-law,* she sternly ordered herself.

"Think about tomorrow. Think about the book," she whispered. She rolled to her side and tucked the covers under her chin. "Think about anything other than Billy Carlton stretched out on your bed making music!"

Eyes squeezed shut, her ears loving the tune coming from above, her mind steadfastly rejected the command. As though she could see through the silver eyes of the unicorn poster across from his bed, she envisioned him sprawled on the pale blue coverlet.

Naked?

Horrified by the explicitness of her imagination, she shouted, "Hey, up there! Knock off the noise!"

The soft notes abruptly ended. The night seemed deadly still with only the muted tones of summer's wilderness song filtering in through the window. Determined to escape the spell of the special brand of music Billy Carlton played, she thumped her pillow.

But sleep wouldn't come. Regardless of how much she silently abused herself for her fit of fanciful dreaming, regardless of how much she punished her pillow for refusing to induce her to sleep, she remained wide awake, eyes staring into blackness. She thought of the lyrics to the golden oldie Billy had been playing: "Mr. Sandman, bring me a dream . . ."

Exhausted but still fighting, she ran through the lyrics and flatly denied them as romantic balderdash. Finally the slowed-down rhythm of the song she silently mouthed seduced her into the irresistible dreamland of sleep, a silver-spangled world where Billy the Kid sang and danced his way throughout the night.

CHAPTER FOUR

An early riser, Christine bounded out of bed smiling. Her sweet dreams couldn't be remembered, but the morning's freshness made her feel joyous.

"Must be the mountain air." She yawned and stretched, unconcerned about the whys of feeling great.

Eager to get started on her tongue-in-cheek manuscript, *Hunting Male Homo Sapiens*, she unpacked a box of spiral notebooks. She pulled out the stacks of notes from several conversations she'd had with Janelle during the past six weeks. Reading the first line of the preface, she grinned.

> The outcome of every hunt depends on three factors: luck, skill, and knowledge. Lady Luck is unpredictable. So is the male of the species. But with proper guidance, the odds of getting the quarry hogtied and brought tamely to the altar dramatically increases.

"Good hook line," she muttered to herself. Picking up a pencil from the nightstand, she tapped her bottom lip thoughtfully.

Her twin had gone into a long spiel about weapons, animal signs, and books she'd need to read. Christine seated herself at the small desk in the corner of her room. Pencil poised, she began applying the skills needed to hunt four-legged animals to hunting the two-legged variety. She began scribbling furiously.

> First, a woman must wield her feminine weapons properly. Each huntress owes it to her quarry and to herself to skillfully use her personal arsenal. The skilled huntress can read signs left by the game. She can stalk quietly through his place of business, or sit motionless within view of the quarry. These skills reduce the dependency on good luck.
>
> There are many ways to obtain knowledge. Studying wildlife in its natural habitat, be it in the courtroom pounding a gavel, or with a stethoscope dangling from around its neck in a hospital, or driving an eighteen-wheeler cross-country, is best but not always possible. Seldom does a huntress have the time or energy for such a costly safari, so she turns to books. Through careful reading, she can benefit from the knowledge and experience of the experts.

"Experts," Christine chortled. She realized she'd have to conduct some interviews with truly experienced women.

"I make my living observing and photographing wildlife under natural conditions in the wilds." The classroom and school corridors could be classified as the wilds. And she did march each class down to the cafeteria to have their pictures taken for the yearbook.

Now to really stretch the truth.

> Living with the creatures I'm studying is the best way to find out what they do at different times of the day, in different seasons, and to learn their reactions to different stimuli.

She tapped her pencil on the bold lie and tried to justify it. Wasn't she living with two men right now? Not exactly in the manner described in the book, but . . . what the heck, Billy Carlton would certainly be considered in the big game category by most women. Maybe she would include a chapter titled Trapping Stars.

Now for the personal touch.

> This book has been compiled for the novice huntress to aid her in identifying, stalking, and capturing the creature known to us as MAN. Add this information to the natural instincts every woman is born with and the knowledge acquired firsthand, then test my techniques against your own. If the book increases the pleasure and success of your ventures into the

wild kingdom, I should receive tons of wedding invitations instead of fan mail.

Knock 'em dead, ladies!

Christine reread her preface and grinned. What red-blooded American woman could resist such a book? None, she answered with confidence. Too bad the bookstores couldn't offer a money-back guarantee with the sale of each book. Or better yet, she mused, discount rates on a honeymoon trip!

Within minutes she wrote a draft that would be acceptable to her sister. She still hadn't had the nerve to bring up to Janelle the change in direction the book would take. The bedroom door opened, distracting her. Janelle strutted in waving a record cover. Hastily Christine closed the notebook.

"Read it and weep," Janelle chirped like the early morning birds she planned on spying on. "Two weeks, right?"

Christine read the small print on the back aloud. " 'Nicolas Gentry, the Friendly Giant, childhood friend, my poetic bodyguard, is to be thanked for making the music come alive with words. Billy.' "

"I'm off to check out his iambic pentameter," Janelle joked. "Don't bother to change the sheets, but do get the woolies out from under the bed."

"Stick around and I'll have you making music instead of writing dirty ditties," Christine suggested good-humoredly.

Janelle chuckled. "I've lived too long not to recognize the matchmaking gleam in your eyes. Forget it. Sharpen your arrows, then aim them at the mirror. I'll be out gathering information for our book."

The door closed quietly behind Janelle.

"That's what I'm afraid of," Christine muttered, pushing her chair back. "Big Nick had better keep his fine-feathered fingers to himself or I'll pluck him beardless."

After taking a quick shower and shampooing her hair, Christine dressed in ragged cutoffs and a shirt several sizes too big. Once she'd rolled her hair up on pink sponge curlers, she decided to get her chores finished before eating breakfast. Fast music increased the speed of getting the work done, so she slid Billy's record *Jump, Shout, Move About* on the turntable of the record player in her sister's room and turned up the volume.

"I ought to short-sheet her bed," Christine shouted over the lyrics. She seriously considered pulling David's favorite prank. There was nothing quite like climbing wearily into bed and finding that your foot only went halfway down the length of the bed. But she decided Janelle would check first. After all, David was her brother too.

Hips bumping and grinding to the throbbing beat of the bass guitar, she imitated the dance steps she'd seen the teenagers do at school. Within seconds she had the bed made. Then she remembered the woolies. Kneeling down, she stuck one leg out, then the other as she copied the sexy ladies doing aerobic exercises.

"No woolies," she yelled gleefully as she shimmied her head and shoulders out from under the bed.

The music abruptly stopped. Billy Carlton, in person, sunglasses in place, a grin tilting his lips, was leaning against the record cabinet. His fingers delicately held the needle off the record. With his other hand he lowered his glasses as he watched Christine shove herself further under the bed.

"How long have you been ogling me?" Christine demanded.

"Long enough to wonder if you're costumed for a space walk," he chuckled. "But not long enough to decipher what 'short-sheet' and 'woolies' are."

Christine yanked at the curlers in her hair with one hand and tugged at her short shorts with the other. "It's rude to enter a bedroom without knocking."

"I knocked. You must not have been able to hear me over this . . . 'noise'?"

Her stomach lurched at the steady diet of her own words. "Good music can be equated to a good book, the operative word being 'good.' What's considered good depends on the reader, or in this case, the listener."

Billy hunkered down at the end of the bed and stuck his head beneath the slats that held up the old-fashioned metal springs. "Was that a compliment?"

"Of sorts," she admitted. The last curler stubbornly refused to untangle from her hair. Christine winced.

"Let me help," Billy offered. He moved closer and reached toward the curler embedded at the crown of her head.

"No, thanks."

Christine could smell the early morning fragrance of a man who had recently showered, shaved, and brushed his teeth. One whiff made her dizzy. She used her elbows to lever herself further away from him.

A woolie was shaken loose from the bed springs. It decorated the golden tan on his right forearm.

Christine picked it off and inspected it. "A fine specimen of a woolie-booger," she explained in the same voice she'd use in the classroom. "I'll show you an example of short-sheeting later."

"You have a very wicked gleam in your eyes," he chided melodically.

"I can't believe you've lived to be thirty-some-odd years old and you've never washed dishes, don't know what a woolie is, and want to have your bed short-sheeted. Were you raised in a hermetically sealed jar?"

Billy removed his reflective glasses and propped his chin on his hand, keeping his head low. "More or less. But I'm willing to swap secrets."

The wistful expression in his eyes touched her heart. "What can you teach a teacher?" she quipped, struggling to verbally push back the urge to reach over and comb her fingers through his hair.

"Hmm," Billy droned thoughtfully. "I know the latest tunes and dance steps, but so do you." He shifted closer until their arms touched, their faces inches apart. "There must be something of value I have to swap."

The minty warmth of his breath washed over her face. Christine inhaled the fragrance as though it were life-sustaining oxygen. His penetrating dark eyes focused on the bottom lip she bit into with her front teeth. Her toes wiggled, a sure sign of anticipation.

"Can you think of anything you'd like?" he crooned with seductive softness, his voice barely above a whisper.

"How are you at kissing?" she blurted, her heart overruling common sense.

Billy's heartbreaking, world-famous grin curved his lips upward. "Fair to middlin'," he answered, using the tip of one finger to investigate the slight cleft in her chin. "I'd hate to disappoint you, though. Grocery store tabloids overrate everything."

"I'll give you an honest rating," she murmured huskily without thinking clearly. Her mind was completely befuddled by his little finger tracing over the pulsating vein in her neck.

Like a pin oak seedling caught in a gentle breeze, his lips seemed to float down on hers for a mere second or two. Christine closed her eyes. The timid kiss reminded her of her first kiss nearly two decades ago. Lips separating, she lightly sighed when his forehead touched hers.

"I'd trade one of my brother's best sharpshooting marbles for another one of those," she confessed solemnly.

"A fair trade," he agreed. He framed her face with both hands. "This could be dangerous," he whispered.

He intended to give her another chaste kiss, but the fire spreading from his chest downward heated the primitive blood pulsating below his waist. There was something precious about the way she parted her lips, trusting him to stop with kisses.

Billy didn't trust himself. Much as he wanted to go back to the uncomplicated days of childhood, the taste of her could easily drive him into a frenzy of adult need. But he couldn't resist exploring the honeyed recesses of her mouth when she fluttered the tip of her tongue against his. His hand twined in the short curls at her nape. He fused their lips in deeper intimacy.

They both must have heard their individual warning systems shrieking, "DANGER. WARNING."

Christine lowered her head to the crook of her arm. The short, broken pants she heard could have been her own, or they could have come from the man who rocked her senses.

"A-plus," she whispered in a strangled voice.

Unable to tolerate the dark seclusion without making an absolute fool of herself, she pushed herself out from under the bed.

Certifiable insanity, she thought. *What on God's green earth am I doing under my sister's bed necking with a rock star? I have to get away from him. Now.*

"I have work to do," she stated firmly. Any excuse for a hasty departure was better than the tense silence in the room.

Knees unsteady, she managed to walk over to the record player. Her hand shook, but she put the diamond needle in the center of the record without scratching it.

A slow, sensuous song about yearning, longing for true love but finding empty loving in one-night stands, made her hand visibly shake. Were the lyrics his or Big Nick's? Mouth dry, she licked her lips. She wanted to ask him, but couldn't.

She crossed to the door and closed it behind her. The temptation to shut the door with her on the inside was almost unbearable.

Billy rolled over and stared at the metal springs. The intensity of his own music, his own words, made his fists clench until his knuckles were white.

Did she purposely put the needle in that particular groove? A scratch the width of the record wouldn't make the muscles in his stomach clench the way "Looking for Love" did.

He'd let too much of himself be exposed to the public with that particular song. But Nick had found the musical score beside his hotel bed and insisted it was too good to be hidden in the stack of unpublished songs he'd written over the years. They argued long and hard until finally Nick threatened to write lyrics unless Billy sold the song or recorded it himself.

How much of your soul can you sell and still survive?

The reason for his "vacation" in the mountains focused in his mind. From early childhood he'd been the darling of the music industry. Child genius, the critics had raved. Both his parents beamed with pride and took a backseat on stage to provide background harmony, to provide parental guidance, to push their star to greater heights. Their son became their sun and everything revolved around him.

He unclenched his hands and felt around on the floor until he found his sunglasses. Out of habit he unfolded the frames and put them on. They protected him from more than bright stage lights. Behind the mirrored lenses he hid the shy eyes of a young boy who much preferred gentle fantasy to the harsh lights of reality.

Grimacing at the irony of life, he realized his limited form of protection had become his trademark. Women, young and old, shrieked with joy when he removed them. Each time he took them off, he sold another piece of his soul for the price of a twenty-five-dollar seat near the stage.

For a relatively short span in his lifelong, all-consuming career, he had defiantly decided to take back part of what he'd given. This song was the end product. Too much booze, too many women, too much luxury, left him emotionally an empty shell, and the fragile shell threatened to crack. He knew it. But his friend Nick had been the one to call a halt to the downhill roller coaster ride.

"I'm gonna get your head screwed on straight if I have to break your damned neck," Nick had blustered.

Nick contacted David, then bodily hauled Billy out of California. First to an isolated island in the Bahamas, then, having been discovered, he arranged for this mountain retreat. Nick wasn't just his bodyguard. He guarded what was left of his soul.

Lithely Billy slid out from under the bed.

Slowly he rose to his feet as he heard the last strains of the ballad. Before the next song began he punched the reject button. The needle scratched against the grooves, then lifted and automatically turned the player off. He sat down on the edge of the bed and raked both hands through his hair.

"Where are the melodies?" he moaned as he tugged at his hair. What happened to the songs he used to hear before he wrote them down? Dammit, he wanted to hear the music!

"Too little, too late," he grumbled, wallowing in self-pity, answering his own question. "Burned out."

Christine entered the room waving a dish

towel to dispel a trace of bluish-black smoke toward the window. "Not burned out, burned up." Billy looked at her as though she were speaking a foreign language. "The eggs. You know . . . food—chomp, chomp. I expected you to come running out of here with a fire extinguisher and spritz the kitchen with foam."

She chuckled and started out the door. When she realized Billy still sat on the edge of the bed practically comatose, she scissored her fingers in front of his eyes to cut through his thoughts.

"Hey, breakfast is ready."

From the dark pit of depression he heard the cheerful inflections in her voice, but it wasn't until she offered her hand that the words registered. Like a blind man grasping for the handle on his trusty seeing-eye dog's harness, he clamped his hand around hers. For some unknown reason he realized Nick could guard what remained of his musical soul, but Christine could restore it.

Laughter bubbled from deep in his chest. "We could go outside with the fire extinguishers and have a blast. I don't think we should mess up the kitchen again."

Hand in hand, they walked into the kitchen. Christine had set the table for four, but only two plates were filled with fluffy scrambled eggs and link sausages. Her eyes gleamed with mischief when they both sat down.

Billy reached for the catsup to pour on his

plate, then stopped mid-motion. "What is that thing in the middle of my eggs?"

"I never welsh on payment. It's a steelie . . . David's best sharpshooting marble," she answered, interspersing the explanation with feminine laughter. "Payment in full for Kiss Number Two."

He picked the steel ball out of his eggs, wiped it off with his napkin, and removed his glasses. "Interested in another trade?"

"Depends," Christine bargained. Could she bargain for temporary custody of his sunglasses? Why had he put them back on? Intuitively she knew his desire to learn the game of marbles wasn't enough to risk losing his glasses.

"What would it take to make you teach me how to use this?"

Christine raised one eyebrow. While she managed to burn the first batch of eggs, she'd done some serious thinking about Billy Carlton, superstar. The man was a bundle of contradictions. He held the music world in his hands, and yet he enjoyed washing a stack of dirty dishes with those same hands. He was a hard-working, realistic multimillionaire, and yet he chose the room decorated with mythical animals to live in. There was no doubt in her mind that his feminine conquests would fill several little black books, and yet he kissed her as though he were unsure of himself.

Half the American population would gladly trade places with her, she sanely rationalized. It didn't mean anything to him. He probably considered it his duty to kiss every woman between the ages of twelve and ninety-nine. Well, she'd had her kiss. Twice was more than enough to convince her he was one variety of the species she was unequipped to handle. Christine swiftly decided some brotherly-sisterly games would defuse the sexual time bomb merrily ticking away inside of her. Better to teach him how to play marbles than to arouse her own hunting instincts.

"You do the dishes and I'll play marbles with you," she glibly replied.

"And here I thought Kiss Three was in the making," he teased, pocketing the steelie and digging into breakfast impatiently.

"You been reading your own press releases? When Kiss Three rolls around I may teach you a thing or two."

Billy tossed his head back and laughed at her presumptuous statement. They both knew he was by far the more experienced. "I'd pay the thousands you mentioned yesterday to test your hypothesis."

"Cheapskate," she scoffed, winking at the same time. "If I could buy you for what you're worth and sell you the next day for what you *think* you're worth, I'd have more money than you do."

"Can you say that three times in a row, real fast, and shoot marbles at the same time?" he asked. His male pride remained intact, unpunctured by her playful barb. "I can."

"Feeling cocky, huh?"

Billy grinned inside and out. "Let's see you do this." He put his fork down and raised his hand. Keeping his fingers straight he bent his little finger at the second knuckle.

She tried to imitate his hand movement, but each time her middle finger and ring finger curled downward also. "I could do it if I really wanted to," she teased, dismissing the feat with a shrug of one shoulder. "I just don't want to."

"Takes practice. Admit you can't do it and I'll let you win at the first game of marbles."

"I don't care if I win or not," Christine said, taking the last bite off her plate.

"Don't tell me you don't care if I take your bag of marbles away from you and traipse off to California."

Christine leaned forward as though about to impart top-secret information. "Why should I care?" She paused dramatically. "They're David's marbles!"

When Janelle and Big Nick walked into the kitchen, Billy had his head flung back, laughing uproariously. The quizzical smile on the huge man's bearded face quietly asked for an explanation, but Billy shook his head in a you-wouldn't-understand gesture.

"See anything of interest out there?" Christine inquired as she reheated the scrambled eggs. She didn't like the secretive smile passing between her twin and Nick.

Janelle poured herself and Nick a cup of coffee. "As a matter of fact, I did. My notebook is half full."

"The preface for the book is completed and in my room." With her face turned toward the white-painted kitchen cabinets she added, "And I cleaned up your room . . . including the woolies."

Billy chuckled. "Maybe you could write a chapter on capturing wild woolies," he suggested straight-faced. " 'Armed with a broom and dustpan, the great female hunter sneaks into the dangerous bedroom. The hunt is on.' " He rose to his feet and tiptoed around the room, searching each nook and cranny.

"Be careful of what you make fun of," Janelle warned. "Remember, the first rule of the hunt is that you have to eat everything you catch."

Christine came close to burning eggs for the second time when Billy wrapped one arm around her waist and began nibbling up and down her neck. His muffled laughter sent chills tumbling down each vertebrae.

"Unless you want egg on your face I suggest you find yourself another woodland species," she threatened in an ominous tone.

The sharp, playful slap on her bare thigh sounded like a rifle shot to her ears. "Gotcha," he murmured. "Are you going to write a chapter on dressing, or in this case, undressing the kill?"

"No," she replied sweetly. "But there is going to be a chapter on the hunter becoming the hunted if you don't get your Hollywood hands away from my Colorado mountains."

Undaunted, Billy circled her waist with both

hands and rubbed his thumbs against her bottom ribs. "Mountain climbing is dangerous but invigorating."

A carefully aimed heel rammed against his shinbone effected an immediate release. Acting as though nothing unusual had happened, Christine strode to the table and served the eggs. Billy hopped around the small room on one foot as though seriously injured, moaning and groaning.

"More coffee?" Christine offered. All eyes except hers were on Billy's antics. "Ignore him. He's practicing a new dance step."

Big Nick raked his fingers over his beard and sighed dramatically as he shook his shaggy head. "Tough rhythm to write lyrics to."

"You're supposed to be my bodyguard," Billy teasingly complained between groans. "Are you going to just sit there while that wildcat breaks my bones?"

Nick forked a bite of eggs into his mouth and chewed thoughtfully. "The twins are a near extinct species on their own territory. I'm adopting a wait-and-watch attitude. I suggest you do the same."

There seemed to be a hidden warning behind his words, but Billy ignored them. Waiting, watching, and wanting were three unaccustomed restraints he hadn't practiced in months. "Come on, Christine," he coaxed. "Let's take a walk on the wild side . . . outside."

"You have kitchen duty, remember?" she reminded him with a saucy smile. "Janelle, when you've finished, why don't we go over your notes?"

"I have a better suggestion," Janelle said, cramming the last bite into her mouth. "Get your notebook and we'll find a tree to lean against and absorb some mountain sunshine while we work."

Within minutes, the right notebook in hand, Christine stepped out on the front porch and inhaled deeply. Billy and Nick, deep in conversation in the kitchen, didn't even notice that she left. "Janelle?"

"Over here," Janelle answered from a boulder where she lay stretched out with a blade of grass stuck between her teeth.

"I've been thinking," Christine said as she took her shoes off and clambered up beside her sister. She heard Janelle groan and plucked the grass from her mouth. "Why couldn't a woman use the same skills to trap a man that a hunter uses to hunt animals? We could write a humorous book on hunting men. Don't more women hunt the two-legged species than the four? What do you think?"

"I think I'm in for trouble if I listen to you."

Christine refused to be discouraged by her initial rejection. "I've jotted down some similarities, and I thought maybe you could test some of my theories out."

Janelle closed her eyes and put her hands over her ears. "I'm not listening to any harebrained schemes you've half hatched. And I refuse to be your guinea pig."

"You don't have to get huffy," Christine retorted, slightly miffed. Here she'd decided to come clean, and Janelle refused to listen.

Rolling to her side, Janelle glared at her sister and shook her head. "If I don't listen, you're going to pout? What's next? A full-fledged tantrum? Banging your heels on stone is going to hurt like hell," she cautioned.

"I don't pout or throw fits"—seeing the woman she'd lived with all her life raise her fair eyebrow, she amended—"anymore."

"Not any less either," Janelle mumbled. "Okay. It's futile to fight with you. Something tells me I'm in for another summer of trouble, but go ahead, spit it out."

Dark eyes shining, smiling broadly, Christine leaned toward her sister and whispered, "How would you like to be the one and only Mrs. Billy Carlton?"

CHAPTER FIVE

Christine could tell from Janelle's hoot of laughter that she hadn't been taken seriously. In a dead level tone she continued, "We'll see who laughs last, sister dear. Listen up. Thanks to my cleverness last night, you have an unrestricted shot at the biggest game around. I've spotted the game, and now we're going to scientifically use instinct and research to bag him."

"Not interested," Janelle protested.

"First we have to research his likes and dislikes. This afternoon I'll make myself scarce while you interview him. You know, have one of those I-want-to-get-to-know-the-real-you-type talks. Here," she said, handing Janelle a list of twenty questions. "Simple, huh?"

Janelle scanned the list. Her mouth formed a small O. "I wouldn't even ask David these questions. Number five is a doozy. 'Do you prefer vamps or virgins?' How am I supposed to bring that topic up in a casual discussion?"

"Be creative. This isn't a detailed lesson plan.

What did you expect? Answers to the questions in the back of a teacher's edition?"

Janelle shook her head in disbelief as she continued to read. " 'Would you marry a woman who says she's carrying your child?' "

"We have to know what he values the most. Wouldn't it be ridiculous to hunt a sparrow with an elephant gun? Well?" Christine could tell by the skeptical expression on her sister's face that she didn't make the connection. "It's the same logic. You wouldn't dress up like a belly dancer and jingle around a man who abhors seeing a belly button."

"Your reasoning is about as clear as the Denver skies during a pollution warning." Janelle read item twenty, wadded the list up, and threw it into a pile of leaves. " 'How long should sex last?' " she quoted.

"Some questions are tougher than others," Christine replied with a smug grin. "I guess you could ask him how long he thinks love lasts. Same thing."

"Love and sex are the same? We need to have a serious talk if you're that confused."

"Once again you can't see the forest for the trees. Isn't it logical to assume that a man who likes quickie sex likes short-term relationships, whereas a man who takes the time to insure his partner of—"

"Hold on. I don't want to hear any more of your offbeat logic." Janelle covered her ears again. "I'll consider changing the thrust of the book to a tongue-in-cheek guide for hunting men, *but . . .* I'm not about to ask a man I met yesterday about his mating habits."

Christine propped herself up on her elbows. "You're determined to end up being a shriveled-up, old maid schoolteacher, aren't you?"

"This isn't the eighteenth century, Christine." Janelle jumped down from the boulder and began walking away. Over her shoulder she tossed, "In case you've forgotten, you're a scant three minutes younger than I am. 'To thine own self be true' *and* practice what you preach."

"What did she mean by those last smart remarks?" Christine muttered, knowing full well what her twin meant. *Some gratitude I get for lending a helping hand. The man of my sister's dreams is holed up here for unknown reasons, within shouting distance, and she doesn't appreciate my efforts to guide her footsteps down the right trail.*

Wouldn't it be fantastic if men were as easy to trap as forest animals? she thought. Lord knows, she'd read phrases like "panther grace," "eyes of a predator," and "mane of hair," often enough. A small smile flickered across her lips. "Pelt of hair on his chest" was her favorite comparison. That was too ridiculous for words. It made chest hairs sound as though they could be used to make a winter coat.

Christine sighed and rolled to her feet. With or without the help of her sister, she would write next year's best seller, she decided as she straightened her shoulders. Novelty with a splash of humor was what the public wanted.

"Anybody ready for a hot game of marbles?" Billy shouted from the front porch in her direction.

Stuck with the complete responsibility for researching the book, she took a giant leap from the boulder. She picked up her shoes, strode to the front of the cabin, and drew a circle with her big toe.

"I've changed my mind about charging you rent. How about candidly answering some questions instead?" she asked boldly.

Billy hooked his thumbs through his front belt loops. "You aren't a disguised reporter for one of those grocery store newspapers we talked about, are you?"

"No," she answered truthfully, watching his luminous gaze flood over her from head to foot. "The editors wouldn't believe someone like you would get mixed up with"—her hands raised from her shoulders and fell to her hips—"a wren."

"With that innocent statement you've convinced me you haven't ever bought one of those yellow rags. Sweetheart, I've 'been seen' leaving the bedrooms of far less attractive women." His canvas shoes soundlessly trod down the wooden steps. In his hand he tossed up a small bag of marbles. Suddenly he lobbed the sack toward her. Caught off-guard, she still managed to catch them. "I'll answer any question you don't mind answering yourself," he bargained, grinning.

Christine cleared her throat at his stipulation. "Too bad you aren't on the negotiating team for the teachers union. I'd be driving a sporty convertible."

"Yes or no?"

Sitting down Indian style, she dumped the contents of the bag on the ground after she raked the fallen leaves from the circle. Billy followed suit. From beneath dark lashes she watched him rub his thumb over the steelie she had given him earlier.

"One question for each marble of yours I knock out of the circle," she renegotiated. Confident that he didn't stand a chance, she added, "And I'll answer a question for every marble *you* knock out of the circle."

"You wouldn't take advantage of an unskilled player, would you?" he teased lightly.

"Who? Me?" she asked in an innocent voice any eighth-grade student would have been proud of. "I'm such a fine teacher I'll have you playing like an expert in no time."

"How about a warm-up game to get me started? Penalty free."

Nodding in agreement, she placed ten marbles in the center of the circle and selected a solid black marble to use as a shooter. "You hold it like this . . ." She demonstrated, making a fist and cocking her thumb behind the black marble. "With a mere flick of the thumb from behind the circle . . ." Three of the ten marbles rolled outside the circle. A cheeky, triumphant grin split her face. "For each marble outside the line you get another turn."

Billy stopped himself from correcting the major bend she made in the rules. Marbles had been one of the few games, other than solitaire card games, he played well. He knew that one player took a shot, then the other player had a turn, but curiosity kept him from correcting her. A devilish gleam lit his dark eyes. Two could play the hustling game as easily as one, he decided as she picked off the remaining seven marbles.

"You make it look easy," he complimented her. "Since you managed to empty the circle without giving me a chance to shoot, how about giving me a couple of warm-up shots?"

"Fair's fair," she readily agreed. Feeling a twinge of guilt about the slight change in the rules, and noticing his awkward grip on the steelie, she magnanimously offered, "I'll give you the edge by letting you break when we play the first game, too."

"You're all heart." Purposely he let the steelie drop off his curved forefinger as his thumb nudged the smooth side. "Any chance of your giving some 'hands-on' tutoring?"

Christine walked on her knees around the circle to his side and wrapped her hand around his. "You can shoot from anywhere behind the line," she murmured, quickly ducking her head and concentrating on teaching him the rudiments rather than looking into his compelling eyes. Her left arm prohibited her from getting close enough to aim his thumb properly.

"Put it around my shoulder," Billy suggested, a smile twitching on his lips.

God, let him be a quick learner, she silently prayed when the side of her breast grazed the bare skin of his forearm.

"It's a matter of balance and aim," she instructed, feeling a bit dizzy. "Put your shooter on your forefinger, then aim your thumb at the one you want to hit."

The steelie rocketed from in front of his thumb, completely jumping over the marbles and landing on the outside of the ring. Christine leaned across the circle and retrieved his shooter. The view of her rounded derrière, the back of her thighs, knees, and calves, proved irresistible to Billy. With a warning chuckle he ran his hand over the backs of her knees.

The light caress resulted in her arm buckling at the elbow and her nose coming dangerously close to the center of the circle before she recovered. She straightened, then hunkered back on her heels.

"Touching the opponent is against the rules," she proclaimed indignantly.

"More rules? I didn't realize a forty-page rule book came with each bag of marbles," he teased.

The gentle rebuke spoken near the crown of her dark curls whispered over her scalp like a sensuous massage. Unable to stop herself, she glanced upward into his intensely dark eyes. *Break every rule,* her libido encouraged. *Push him backward, pin his hands over his head, and kiss him until the amused light in his eyes flares with desire. Completely unbutton his shirt and nuzzle against his golden chest hairs.* She could hear her own heartbeat thudding in her chest like a wild bird trapped in a cage.

"You've got the hang of it," she mumbled, drawing rein on her runaway fantasy and moving to the right to put space between them.

Billy audibly released the breath he'd been holding as he read her silent message. For a fraction of a second he thought he'd seen a wistful look in her eyes. But he must have been mistaken. He hunched into shooting position, wondering if the string of notes he heard were coming from the birds in the surrounding forest, or if the melodic tones echoed from his own head.

"Take a few practice shots," she advised, struggling to quell her shaky fingers by tossing the steelie in front of his knees and briskly rubbing both palms over the fronts of her legs.

"Here goes nothing," Billy replied, picking up his shooter and carelessly aiming.

Get your mind on your business, Christine silently berated herself. *Get ready to quiz him.* Her determination to find out information for the book resembled the wadded paper by the boulder: completely crumpled, unreadable.

"We might as well get started. Hopefully

competition will take the square edges off my steelie. I'll break."

Hunkered down, Billy aimed, cocked his thumb, and used enough force to barely spread the marbles apart. One marble lazily rolled outside the circle. "Great!" he enthused. "My question?"

"Ask away," Christine grimaced with mock ferocity.

"Why aren't you married?"

Christine retorted, "Mr. Right hasn't asked."

Accepting her flip answer, he took another turn and edged another marble outside the circle. "Describe what you think Mr. Right looks like."

Blond hair, penetrating black eyes, sensuous mouth, she thought as she said, "Latin men are a turn-on."

Billy raked his fingers through his blond hair and muttered, "I guess I could dye my hair and take Spanish lessons."

He picked up the green marble from outside the circle and decided to let her have a shot. On purpose he scattered the marbles, but none of them rolled outside the boundary. "Your turn."

Grinning, Christine set her fist behind the circle and fired away. Two marbles spun out of the circle.

"Two questions." Remembering the rules for designing a good test, she started out with simple questions. "Do gentlemen prefer blondes?"

"The dark coloring of Latin women is a turn-on," he replied honestly. His eyes swept from her dark hair to her brown eyes.

"Why aren't you married?"

"Ms. Right hasn't asked," he replied with a chuckle.

Christine snorted at his liberal attitude and took another shot. Three marbles jetted out.

"Name three places a woman can meet an attractive man."

"You're bending the rules again, but I'll answer your *three* questions." He sat back, folding his legs in front of him. "A male striptease joint?"

Laughing, Christine shook her head at his twisted interpretation of the question.

"On a California beach? At a music concert." The last reply was spoken in a soft crooning tone.

Christine squirmed uncomfortably. Knees digging into the soft dust, she blurted out the next question, the one Janelle swore she would never ask a man.

"Do you prefer virgins or experienced women?"

"Which category are you in?" Billy quizzed, breaking all the rules.

"Play fair. You didn't knock a marble out."

Billy knew this was a do-you-still-beat-your-wife question. Should he say virgin, and Christine wasn't, he expressed a double-standard viewpoint he didn't believe. Should he answer experienced, she could construe it as a preference for kinky Hollywood orgies.

"Before I answer I want to remind you that I'm entitled to the same question the next time I win a marble." The cocky grin she bedazzled him with assured him she had her answer ready. He searched his mind for an evasive reply. When he thought of one he mirrored her smile and said, "A promiscuous virgin."

"No such animal," Christine shot back, admiring his quick wit.

"Three marbles left and they're spread out. Take careful aim, lady, because I'm thinking up some mind-blowing questions."

"Oh, yeah? In that case I won't bother with any more easy questions." Christine took two shots and knocked two marbles out, but on the third shot, as she bent over to get into the best position, Billy gave a loud wolf whistle that spoiled her aim. She missed.

"I didn't touch," he said defensively. His hands hovered over the curves of her stretched-out body, close but not touching. "Obviously you didn't impose enough restrictions."

"Are you always such a rascal?" she asked, chuckling, wasting a question.

"Yes. One more, sweetheart, then it's my turn."

Certain his expertise wasn't up to making the shot, Christine rolled the tip of her tongue around the side of her mouth. "How long does love last?" She couldn't bring herself to say the words lust or sex. She watched his eyes narrow, his fingers stroke the round sharpshooter.

He answered with sincerity. "Nick's lyrics say the love between man and woman lasts forever." He closed his eyes and raised his head until he felt the sun's rays on his face. Through tight lips he voiced a thought he'd kept hidden too long. "Parental love can be too strong, last too long. It can choke." He shook his head to dispel the gray cloud threatening to block the sun. "Sweetheart, I can't answer questions I can't comprehend."

Her mouth suddenly became dry. She'd peeked behind the mask of humor he'd been wearing and seen a rare glimpse of a strong man, the heartthrob of millions of women, who had never experienced love. She swallowed the lump of sadness she felt. She wanted to comfort him, give him an optimistic piece of advice, but she couldn't think of any. Should he ask the same question of her, should she reply with the same sincerity? She didn't know how long love lasted.

Infatuation lasted as long as it took to make the conquest. Puppy love lasted throughout teenage years. Lust? Only until the sheets had been changed.

When Billy lowered his head, he cupped the side of her face with one hand, rejecting the pity he saw in her eyes. "Ask me when I'm wearing my sunglasses and I'll give the answer reporters prefer."

"Which is?"

"An old Chinese proverb confuses love with sex. 'The meal isn't over until everyone has gotten their fortune cookies.'" His lips twisted into a grim smile. "You aren't laughing."

"I'm not amused," she replied, wanting to reach out and wrap her arms around him, wanting to feel his arms draw her close.

His thumb traced a path over her cheekbones to her full lower lip. His heartbeat matched the increasing pace of her pulse, which he felt as it throbbed at the base of her throat. *Can this teacher teach a slow learner how to love?* The beginning strains of the tune he heard earlier wafted illusively through his mind. He swayed closer, ears attuned for more than the beginning measures of a slow ballad. He saw a flicker of wariness in her eyes, breaking the melody.

"I won't hurt you," he reassured her, lacing his fingers between hers and rising to his feet. "Come with me."

As though mesmerized by the need she saw in his dark, soulful eyes, she followed him without hesitation. They entered the forest, but she didn't notice the dimming light. Soft pine needles, dried leaves crunched under her bare feet; she didn't feel them. The pungent smell of the forest was faint compared to the fragrance of desire blooming in the space between their bodies. Seconds could have been minutes, hours; Christine lost track of space and time.

She followed the soft humming sound coming from between Billy's half-smiling lips. She clung to the hand guiding her into the unknown. She didn't question; he didn't question. There were no answers, only the sweet yearnings they both felt.

Once they entered a small glade, he unbuttoned his shirt and placed it on the thick carpet of grass beneath the cathedral of branches. His dark eyes locked on the golden fires emanating from her brown eyes, a warmth broke through the fragile barrier of skin and flesh and warmed him to the marrow.

"I can't promise . . . forever," he murmured, answering the hidden questions he saw as he unbuttoned her shirt, pulling her against his chest. "Only a here-and-now love. Is that enough for you?"

He sank to his knees, taking her with him. Protecting her from the scraps of errant leaves and twigs, he gently laid her in the warmth of his own shirt, efficiently ridding them of their clothing as he listened for her thoughtful reply.

"It's more than I've ever known," Christine answered, accepting his terms unequivocally. "Maybe more than we'll ever have again."

"Then love me, sweetheart, here, now, and I'll love you."

His lips closed over hers with the same tentativeness of their second kiss. More gently than the summer breeze caressing the treetops, he traced the bow of her lower lip with the tip of his tongue. As though he held the secret golden key, she parted them, allowing him inside.

She nudged one leg between his thighs until they twined intimately from tongue to toe. The rules, the book, fled to the dark corners of her mind as she closed her eyes and concentrated on the sensation of touch. A sixth sense told her of the restraint he placed on himself. Or was it the tense bunching of the muscles on his back that contrasted with the languid nibbles his lips made as they covered the planes of her face? Or could it be his hands skimming down the sensitive skin between her breasts to lush, dark curls, but stopping, traveling back to the twin hardening mounds and convulsively kneading them until her nipples became hard?

She shifted to her side, inching her knee back and forth along the outside of his thigh as he lowered his head to moistly kiss one breast, then the other. Her back arched when he confined himself to sipping the tips; she begged for the heat of his mouth to suckle deeply by embracing his fair head closer. A deep satisfying moan passed through her lips when he obliged, drawing the tight bud into the swirling hot vortex of his mouth.

Billy unconsciously drew five lines, a staff, from one fragile hipbone to another and painted languorous half and whole notes across her aroused heated flesh. With each note humming in his mind, the beat of his heart marked time louder than a bass drum. The stems of the treble notes pointed toward each breast he lavishly kissed; the stems of the bass notes directed him downward to the secret music throbbing from the depths of her femininity.

Timidly, afraid the song coming from his soul would cease to flood his senses, he parted the tangle of feminine hair. He caressed her as she moaned beneath his touch with abandon.

Amazed, he pressed his ear against her chest. Was the syncopated music coming from himself or from Christine? He captured her lips fervently, passionately, to seal the song in his memory.

Christine moved against his hand. The fiery passion of his plunging tongue warned her of his rampant desire. She parted her thighs, urged him to seek and fill, touch and stroke, take her beyond the boundaries of earth's mountains to higher peaks. Her fingers sought and found him. As though in close harmony she matched his stroking tongue with her hand.

"I've waited so long to end the silence," he crooned against her lips.

She heard the strange, nonsensical love words but was past questioning their meaning. In short panting spurts she murmured incoherent phrases of her own.

Billy moved over her, watching the undulating motions of her body, waiting to savor every moment before he brought her to complete fulfillment.

Christine opened her eyes, her look questioning his hesitation. "Yes, oh please, yes," she whispered, encouraging him, guiding him. Her dark eyes implored him to follow the path that twisted and circled, taking both of them beyond the exquisite torture.

The pulsating pagan drums of primitive music pounded in his head. He plunged deep within in one swift, sure stroke. Uncertain he could keep pace with the throbbing drums without ending the song too quickly, Billy gulped air into his lungs to slow the building crescendo.

Shaking her head from side to side, Christine ground herself against him to break the bonds of constraint. She wanted to soar to the pinnacle of their passion. Her hands gripped the constricted muscles of his forearms; her slender legs wrapped around his hips. Her teeth sank into her lower lip in the agony of waiting.

As though a coda sign returned him to the beginning chorus, in his mind he hummed soft whole notes. His vocal chords ached to vibrate with the profound emotion locked inside him. Sad minor chords changed to moderately slow major chords with each thrust. The melody swelled, but he silently sustained the low notes, reached for the high ones.

He made love to Christine with the same intense concentration he used while performing in front of thousands of applauding, cheering fans. Nothing could distract him from conveying his song, his love. A burst of joy exploded within him when the final note was sung, then echoed and faded into satiated silence.

Christine wiped the thin sheen of perspiration off his forehead, off his curved upper lip when he snuggled against the crook of her neck. His heated breath lightly blew over the flushed skin above her breasts.

"I'm exhausted," he mumbled, tasting the salt on his lips, "but . . ." He tried to explain the high he felt after a successful concert and couldn't. Only a performer could understand the pumping adrenaline in his bloodstream even though his body sagged from tiredness.

She smiled at his inability to express what he felt. Normally she could verbalize her feelings about everything, yet what she felt now was too special, too wonderful for words.

"I know," she whispered. And she did.

CHAPTER SIX

"Do you always hum after making love?" Christine teased in an impish voice after they had returned to the site of the cabin. She had quickly stooped down and blasted the lone marble out of the circle in one accurate shot.

Billy grinned as he hunkered down beside her. "You twisted the rules in your favor again. I seem to recall it being my turn."

"Just answer the question, Mr. Carlton." Her eyes twinkled with mischievous curiosity.

"Put the marbles back in the circle and I'll answer your question," he bargained.

Christine scrambled around the outskirts of the ring, plopped the marbles in the center, then eased herself next to him with an expectant expression clearly visible on her face.

"I haven't composed a song in months."

"I could swear you were humming," she protested.

Billy sealed her argumentative mouth with a hard kiss. "While I was lying in your arms I remembered a few bars of what you say you heard, but I know if I got out a piece of staff paper I wouldn't be able to write it down."

She saw the sad, wistful smile on his lips. Her heart went out to him. How frustrating it must be for a man who composed some of the most popular songs of the decade not to be able to string the notes together.

"Writers call it writer's block; teachers call it burnout. Three of our staff didn't sign a contract for next fall," she mused aloud. Realizing she had put the kiss of death on his career with the comparison, she tried to cover up the faux pas. "But your fans love the way you sing and dance, not your songs."

Bumble mouth! Give his career a smacking loud kiss of death, then blithely tell him the fans aren't concerned with the creative part of his music making.

Seeing her face turn bright red, Billy decided to make a joke of her comments by clutching at his heart and keeling over backward. "One more stab ought to finish me off," he groaned, chuckling.

"Dammit, you know what I mean. People flock to your concerts. Most of them don't read the program to find out who wrote the music or the lyrics."

"No printed programs at rock concerts." He laughed as he let out a lingering groan. "The lady hates light rock."

"One of your albums is up in my room right now," she argued. A glimmer of an idea lit up her face. "I have a tape recorder up there too.

What do you think about making love with the recorder on?"

"And they say Hollywood is decadent," he teased. "Music is like inspiration; it's spontaneous. We might make love a thousand times and the only thing to play back would be . . ." He reached up and pulled her down on top of him. Leering, he whispered, "The sound of my lips slurping. Or those purring noises you make when you're aroused."

"Shut up." Christine clamped her hand firmly over his mouth. "What a despicable way to talk to a schoolmarm."

"The singer and the schoolmarm—what an improbable combination," he mumbled between her fingers. "Do you think we could cut a record together? I can see it all now . . ."

"Don't you dare tell me what you see!"

"Why not? I'll bet you had some X-rated questions you wanted to ask me this morning, didn't you?" Swift as a mountain cat he pushed her to her side and sprawled on top of her. "Don't take time to think up an evasive answer."

Hands pinned above her head, Christine pressed her lips shut and refused to answer.

"Christine Mc Mahon, answer the question!" he demanded, lightly shaking her by the wrists.

"I'm not answering any questions unless they are a penalty for losing a marble," she replied primly. "I bend the rules a bit, but you corkscrew them!"

Three seconds later Billy hunched over the circle, and within fifteen seconds he knocked all ten marbles well outside the edge. Christine couldn't believe her eyes. He made her look like a first grader taking college entrance exams.

"You cheated!" she protested when he turned around; his black eyes gleaming with triumph. "You hustled me!"

"Baby doll, you need to look in a mirror before you send me to the school principal. You owe me responses to ten questions. And you damned well better shoot straight this time."

Christine reached over his shoulder and took his aviator glasses out of his front pocket. Mutinous thoughts racing through her mind, she perched them on her nose. "Fire away, marblesharp."

"Why did you play the reluctant virgin about sharing the cabin?" he asked. Gone was the boyish, lopsided grin, the charm. Instead a thin-lipped predator, poised to attack, confronted her. "You have a devious reason behind your less than gracious acceptance of Nick and me. What is it?"

"You wouldn't believe the truth if you heard it."

"Try me," he suggested grimly, grabbing her ankle when she started to get up. Much as he preferred to be blinded to life's realities, he didn't want the answers to his questions appearing in an article in the *Rocky Mountain Times*. Was she stringing him along, planning to hop from the classroom to a newspaper office? Any paper in the nation would pay several thousand dollars for an exclusive interview with Billy the Kid. He dreaded hearing the worst possible answer, but he was prepared. Disillusionment followed him everywhere he went like a gray shadow.

She peeled his fingers off her ankle using her sharp fingernails when necessary. "Considering what happened in the glade, you're going to think I made this up," she warned as she heaved herself upward, careful to stay out of his reach.

"Quit procrastinating," he ordered.

"I thought you'd make an ideal husband for Janelle."

"For Janelle? Are you crazy? Why?" he asked, each query a bit louder than the previous one.

"Yes, for Janelle." A spunky grin curved her lips upward. "I must be a bit crazy around the edges when you consider I made love with my prospective brother-in-law. And"—she shrugged—"you and Janelle look perfect together."

"Janelle and I?" he repeated, not certain she wasn't pulling his leg.

"Yeah. Both blond. Both beautiful. Surely you remember the pep talk I gave you in the kitchen."

"When you were washing dishes?"

"Uh-huh."

"You were playing matchmaker for your twin and myself?"

Christine removed the sunglasses. She twirled them around by the earpiece, folded them shut, and tossed them in his direction. "You must need these to hear with. You wasted eight of your ten questions," she stated smugly, turning toward the front door.

"Where do you think you're going?" he demanded, catching up to her with two long strides. "You can't saunter away from me when we're in the middle of a knock-down-drag-out."

"Oh, but I can. Watch me. I'm going inside to work." She took the porch steps two at a time. Billy halted at the bottom. "Don't plan on me asking for a rematch," she tossed over her shoulder.

"Keep in mind that I have one question left," he crooned melodically.

Christine chuckled. "You'll waste it on something inane," she scoffed, opening the door.

"Not this time, sweetheart."

A shiver ran up her spine when she saw him put his glasses back in place. Once they were perched on his nose his mood switched from friendly to defensive to bordering on antagonistic.

"Moody musician," she mumbled to herself.

She could hear Nick and Janelle in the kitchen talking and laughing. She needed privacy. Her world seemed to have stopped its orderly rotation and spun off into the dark unknown. Billy's reaction to why she hadn't put up a stronger fight about sharing the cabin both amused and confused her. Didn't he see the obvious? Janelle would make an ideal wife.

Closing the bedroom door, she lay down on the bed and stared at the ceiling. Mentally she drew a dark line down the center of the white space. On one side she scrawled "Janelle," on the other side "Christine."

Listing her sister's attributes was simple. Tall. Blond. A-plus student. Beautiful. Loving. Even-tempered. Sane. Good maternal instincts.

Under her own name she mentally jotted: Short. Dark. Average. Average. Loving. Mercurial temperament. Slightly crazy around the edges. Question mark.

Who in his right mind would put a gold star by my name? The irrefutable choice would be Janelle.

Why me? she wondered. *Why am I the one who hiked off into the forest with him?*

It was too bad he couldn't remember the tune he hummed. It was imprinted on her mind. In an off-key voice she tried to reproduce the notes. She glanced back up at the ceiling and added "Can't carry a tune in a bucket" beneath her name. Janelle could sing like a lark in mating season. Christine could hear the music in her mind, but once the notes went past her lips the song was a lost cause.

"That's just what Billy Carlton needs," she grumbled aloud, "a tone-deaf wren."

She closed her eyes but couldn't rest. As she silently cursed the cause of her frustration, she heard the door upstairs close. The bedsprings squeaked noisily. For a moment she didn't recognize the song Billy strummed on his guitar. When she realized he was singing "Feel Like Makin' Love" she felt like confessing at the top of her lungs the title of another hit song, "Nobody Does It Better."

On the television music station she had seen him perform the song in front of a throng of females shouting, "Yes, yes, yes!" At the time she had been amused by foolish women reaching toward the stage. They might as well have been reaching for the moon, she remembered thinking. Billy hadn't missed a beat, hadn't smiled, hadn't encouraged their vows of undying love.

Disgruntled, angry with her lack of control, she realized Billy Carlton probably wreaked havoc on every woman's nerves. She also admitted she was caught between wanting to hug him close and wanting to drive him to his knees.

The tune from above abruptly ended.

Stop daydreaming, she told herself in the same stern voice she used in the classroom. *You can't catch a star either!*

She got up and went over to her desk. The spiral notebooks lay in front of her. She understood the teenage preference to doodle the latest heartthrob's name all over the cover instead of paying attention to her lectures.

Unable to resist, Christine picked a red pencil out of the desk drawer and drew a heart interlocked with a star on the front cover. In block letters she printed C.M.M. on the heart; in the star she wrote B.C. Exasperated at giving in to such an immature urge, she put a heavy X on the drawing.

Janelle barged in without knocking. "Nick and I are going out again. You want to tag along?"

Covering the doodle with her hand, Christine shook her head. "You can't go. It's your turn to cook dinner. Why don't you get started frying the chicken while Nick and I go for a walk? Did you show him the cave?"

The door slammed. "What are you up to now?"

"Me? Nothing. Honest."

"Is this another one of your attempts to throw Billy and myself together? Give it up! He's more interested in you than he is in me."

"You think so?" A strong dose of happiness bubbled through her bloodstream.

Janelle groaned. "Don't tell me you've fallen for his Hollywood charm. Do you know why he's here?"

"Burnout."

"The only thing he burned out was the steel teeth in his zipper. The man has been on a sex binge, according to Nick. All a woman has to do is say yes, and she'll find herself on her back with Billy Carlton blanketing her." Janelle pointed her finger, then shook it in typical schoolmarm fashion. "You be careful around him."

Too late, Christine silently thought, hiding the blush tingeing her cheeks by averting her head. *Good thing the school board did away with tall stools and dunce caps.*

"Nothing like having your best friend mouthing slander," Christine blurted in defense of Billy.

"Define slander. It's spoken untruths. Nick jerked Billy out of California because his escapades threatened his career. The reason they're both brown as berries is because they spent two months in the Bahamas." Janelle defended Nick with the same vehemence her twin protected Billy. "Nick should have left him there, but he didn't. When the groupies began to gather he called David. That's how they ended up here."

"Nick thought we were groupies when we showed up, remember?" Christine murmured as she recalled the scuffle on the front porch.

"He's at the end of his tether. I've convinced Nick we're both too sensible to get involved with a rock star. I would have warned you this morning, but I didn't find out the gruesome facts myself until after breakfast. When I checked on you, the two of you were shooting marbles in front of the cabin. Don't let him get you alone. No telling what he'll pull," Janelle warned.

"Could Nick have exaggerated?" Christine asked, throwing up her last line of defense.

Janelle tapped her foot on the floor, impatient with her twin's bullheadedness. "You talk to Nick. Afterward I want your promise to be careful around Billy."

Christine blinked to keep the tears from slithering down her cheeks. "Can you keep Billy at bay while we're gone?"

"He'll be shipped back to California in pieces if he tries anything with me," Janelle promised grimly. "And if he tries anything with you, the pieces won't be big enough to wrap. I'm a history teacher, but I don't find anything romantic about a twentieth-century rake."

Any urge to confide in her sister was stifled by the expression she saw on Janelle's face. Forcing the corners of her mouth to turn upward, Christine attempted to laugh off the sinking sensation in the pit of her stomach. "We'll consider ourselves 'posted property.' Maybe we should put signs on the outside of the bedroom doors that say TRESPASSERS WILL BE SHOT."

Chuckling at Christine's natural affinity for making something funny out of dead serious topics, Janelle moved back to the door. "Come on, Little Red Riding Hood. I'll protect you from the Big Bad Wolf."

"Are you certain I'm safe going off into the woods with the wolf's best friend? He still reminds me of a huge, hairy bear," Christine teased as she joined her sister.

"Trust my hunting instincts," Janelle

quipped, hugging Christine. "A bear isn't as treacherous as a wolf."

"When Nick starts calling one of us 'honey,' we post the signs," Christine retorted. "Funny, I don't remember these woods being overpopulated with wild game when we were kids.

"Beware of the wolf in sheep's clothing," she whispered as they entered the living room.

Nick's bulk blocked the sunlight coming through the front screen. "You ready for exploring?" he asked Janelle.

"I'm on the dinner shift. Christine will show you the cave." Janelle shot him a meaningful look. "She's anxious for you to tell her everything you know . . . about getting published."

His eyes narrowed perceptibly. "Okay, I'll take the pill with me."

"What kind of pills are you on?" Christine asked, leading the way up the trail behind the cabin. A rake and a druggie. David should have left the dynamic duo in the Bahamas. Neither of them belonged in the fresh mountain air of Colorado.

"You're the pill," Nick drawled with a chuckle to take the sting out of the insult.

Christine audibly gasped. "Thanks a lot," she snapped sarcastically. "Keep in mind that medicine can be good or bad under *normal* conditions."

"From the shenanigans you manage to embroil your sister in, my guess is you'd be nothing but bad medicine for Billy Carlton."

"Don't let being polite interfere with saying what you think," she retorted. Christine held back the low branch of a pine until Big Nick was smack-dab in the middle of the path, then she let it go. "Sorry."

Nick broke the impact of the branch with his forearm. "You remind me of a Texas fire ant: small, but armed with teeth and a stinger. Don't take this personally, but Billy doesn't need any woman messing up his life."

Sidestepping a low-growing thorny shrub, Christine smiled when she heard him suck air into his lungs rather than voice a loud "ouch."

"I hope your poetry is sweeter than your prose. Billy isn't a kid."

"No? I'd say his time clock is running backward. He was a hard-working, tough businessman until a year ago. That's when he reverted to being a horny teenager. And now? Do you honestly consider playing marbles an adult activity?"

"Depends on what you play for."

"Please," Nick protested when he saw her catch another branch.

Christine smiled sweetly, holding the branch until he was beside her.

"Were you playing spin the bottle with marbles instead of a milk bottle?" Nick asked.

"Kisses weren't the object of the game if that's what you're inferring," she replied indignantly. "The loser had to answer a question."

"Janelle told me about your change in plans for the masterpiece of literature you're writing, also about the questions you wanted her to ask Billy. I'd think an English major, especially a teacher, would be more interested in writing the great American novel."

"Why aim for the impossible? I'm writing to sell." She wheeled around when she heard him laughing softly. "What's so funny?"

"Don't you think setting your sights on Billy Carlton is aiming a bit high?"

"Finally we agree. While I was in my room I listed my deficiencies"—she paused long enough to watch him nod in agreement, then added in a devilish tone—"and Janelle's attributes."

The surprise attack failed miserably. Nick tossed back his head and laughed uproariously. "Janelle said you had armed yourself with bow and arrow for the role of Cupid. Forget it. She isn't interested."

"The summer isn't over yet," Christine cautioned, turning her head to see his reaction.

"Watch your step!" He grabbed her arms to keep her from falling over a rock in the middle of the path. "You're going to break your neck if you don't watch where you're going."

Christine clamped her lips together and twisted out of his hold. Did he intend his warning to have a double meaning? Instead of *neck*, did he really mean *heart?* She glanced up, trying to detect any hidden meaning lurking in his eyes.

"I'm going to protect you . . . from Billy, from yourself," he stated unequivocally. "For good measure, I'll volunteer to help with the manuscript."

The ineffective bravado of her threat bounced back in her face. Christine sank to the rounded surface of the rock she'd nearly tripped over. Nick clearly had everything under control.

As he sat down beside her, she wondered if the rock were symbolic of Billy Carlton's popping up in her life. Had the Fates put Big Nick in the picture to keep her from falling for Billy the same way he kept her from stumbling on the rock?

Inwardly Christine grimaced at the comparison. The Fates' timing was off. Nick should have warned her earlier. Because she'd already fallen. Now she had to ignore the pain, pick up the pieces, and go on as though uninjured.

"Are you going to tell Billy you've warned us?" Christine asked, her pride smarting under his close scrutiny.

"Depends on you," he replied with a slight shrug. "He's close to recuperation. I heard him picking at the guitar last night and again this morning. He hasn't touched it for months. I'm not going to play the heavy between you two unless you make me."

Christine bit her tongue to keep from blurting out, "He hummed a new song after we made love. You could be wrong. I may be good medicine for him." Instead she lowered her head, pretending to remove a hangnail on the cuticle of her thumb. She couldn't reveal the intimacies she and Billy had shared to Big Nick any more than she could to her twin sister.

"You think time is the cure? Why not—"

"Love? Billy doesn't know what love is. In his book, love strangulates."

Christine remembered Billy's own words: "Love can choke." Slowly nodding her head, she couldn't argue the point.

"He needs a friend, not a lover." Nick placed her hand in his. The tips of her short fingers barely reached the first joint. "Can you be a friend?"

"A playmate?"

"In the most platonic sense of the word, yes. You have a unique talent for making him laugh. Use it." Nick glanced at her watch. "How much further to the cave?"

"Another fifteen or twenty minutes," she replied, mutely digesting the confidences Nick shared.

Her heart wrenched as though Nick had squeezed it with his powerful hand. The pain stripped away any delusions about their lovemaking. She could love Billy Carlton far beyond the here and now she promised. But the stipulation of here and now for him was an escape clause.

"We'd better head back. Janelle will have dinner ready." Nick straightened. Still holding her hand he pulled her up beside him. "Don't peg me as the villain, Christine. I'll be the best man at his wedding when he finds the right woman."

"I knew I wasn't the right woman from the beginning," she admitted lightly. "Now I know Janelle isn't either."

"I've convinced Janelle of the salability of the woman-hunting-a-man idea. Do you want my input?"

"You want to help?" she asked, relieved by his timely change of topic.

He nodded.

"Thanks." Poking him in the ribs, she teased, "After this one hits the best seller list, we'll coauthor the great American novel."

Chuckling at the common dream of most authors, he further justified his offer to help by saying, "A man should have input into a book about hunting."

"How would a woman go about capturing a bear of a man such as yourself?" Happily she switched to this safe topic of discussion.

"Catch him in the winter when he's roly-poly fat and ready to hibernate."

"Bears hibernate in caves. Do they check them out in the summertime?" she kidded. "Stock them with honey and nuts?"

"Watch your sassy tongue, honey. Janelle has already told me you're nuts." With the skill of an experienced wordsmith he twisted his words as he smacked his lips.

"I'm saner than I'm given credit for," Christine retorted.

Nick stopped her as she turned to retrace

their steps. "You have a special gift you can give Billy."

She cocked her head quizzically.

"Laughter. Keep 'em smilin', eh?"

CHAPTER SEVEN

"Want to sleep in your own bedroom tonight?" Billy asked her later when Janelle was in the kitchen getting a bag of marshmallows and Nick was looking for long sticks to use to roast them over an open fire.

Keep 'em smilin', she reminded herself, trying to stay on the opposite side of the circle of stones they worked on in preparation for building a fire. *Be friendly, but aloof.*

"What's wrong? Scared of the unicorns on the walls?" she teased.

Nick strode toward them from the edge of the thicket.

"Meet me out here when they've gone to bed," Billy muttered, trying to keep Nick from overhearing their conversation.

"These should do the trick," Nick announced, waving the foot-long sticks. He glanced at Christine meaningfully. "I wouldn't want anyone to burn their fingers."

Janelle bounded down the front steps. "Good timing. Here are the marshmallows and Billy's guitar."

As though the seating had been preassigned, Nick sat down between Christine and Billy on one side, and Janelle did the same on the other side.

"I thought you two would have the fire started by now," Janelle complained with a what-were-you-doing look cast toward her twin.

"Christine took forever gathering wood," Billy answered as he struck a match to the kindling.

Janelle and Nick grinned as Christine retorted, "You have to be careful out there after dark. Don't you know about the snakes and furry critters on the move once the sun goes down?" she asked in a patronizing manner.

"I'll go with you next time," Billy offered. "We can't have a sweet thing like you picking up a snake instead of a stick, now, can we?"

When he leaned toward the fire the orange-red flames distorted his comical leer into a sinister grin. It left little doubt in Christine's mind that he could think of far less perilous things for her hands to be doing. Pasting a smile on her face she busied herself by jabbing a marshmallow onto the stick Nick handed her. Hopefully by ignoring the comment it would go away. She poked her marshmallow directly into the fire.

"You're supposed to wait until the fire burns down some, aren't you?" Billy pointed out when the flames charred the marshmallow immediately.

Janelle laughed. "She's impetuous as usual. Our whole family used to eat burnt offerings off her stick rather than waste them."

"Why don't you sit by me?" Billy suggested, patting the ground next to his lean hips. "I like things crisp on the outside and hot and sweet on the inside."

None of them missed the innuendo. Nick reached over, covering the flustered look on Christine's face by barely twitching the end of her stick until the black glob dropped into the fire.

"Why don't you give us a rousing rendition of 'Heartbreaker' while we wait for the fire to get just right?" Nick suggested.

Christine's mind spun as she tried to keep up with the underlying messages the four of them were sending. Billy picked up the guitar, strummed a few chords of his award-winning song, hesitated, then slowly began picking out the tune he'd hummed when he was with Christine in the glade.

Nick's jaw dropped. "Is that new?"

Nodding, Billy leveled his dark eyes in Christine's direction. "I'm working on it, but I don't have it perfected yet."

"Maybe it needs a snappier rhythm," Nick innocently suggested.

Billy gave Nick the warm, lopsided smile that when on the covers of music magazines, made them sell like crazy. "It ends with a pounding, primitive, syncopated beat." He illustrated what he meant by beating his fourth and fifth fingers against the base of the guitar as he increased the volume and pace of the music.

Janelle clapped enthusiastically when he abruptly stopped. "It's different from anything you've done before, isn't it?"

"Uh-huh," he nodded. "Have you heard anything before like this?" he casually asked Christine.

Nick, excitement evident in his voice, roared, "Man, it's fantastic! A blend of the sweet mystery of innocence and savage fundamentals. What kind of lyrics did you have in mind?"

"What kind of words would you recommend, English teacher?" he quizzed softly, seductively.

All eyes were on her expectantly. The back of her head began pounding with a thudding ache.

The advice Nick sagely gave about keeping Billy laughing was easier said than done. If she closed her eyes while he played, she could have conjured up a scene that would have made Nick blush to the roots of his dark beard. Or singe it off completely, she thought.

Unable to think of anything clever or witty, she jumped to her feet, swaying dizzily. With both hands pressed against her temples, she groaned aloud. "I'm going to have to call it a night. My head is pounding."

"Can I get you something for it?" Billy asked.

Another double entendre? "No, thanks. I'll be all right once I'm in bed." Her face paled when she realized the way that could be misconstrued. "So long. See you in the morning."

As she escaped from the heat of the flames, away from the glowing fires in Billy's dark eyes, she heard Nick detain Billy by exclaiming exuberantly, " 'So Long.' That's a flashy title. I could make the ballad portion of the song with the wistful meaning of 'so long.' You know—'It's been so long since I've been with you.' Then, when the beat changes, change the meaning—'So long, baby, it's been fabulous, but a singin' man has to keep traveling.' What do you think?"

Christine softly closed the screen door behind her. With long strides she moved through the dark living room into the kitchen. Her eyes blinked painfully when she flipped on the overhead light. Momentarily they seemed unable to focus. She filled the glass by the sink with water, then began scrounging around in the cabinet for aspirin.

"Let me help," she heard from the doorway.

Before she could voice a protest, Billy moved behind her, lightly massaging the back of her neck with one hand as he moved the bottles around on the shelf with the other. When he found the aspirin he asked, "How old are these?"

With his hand on the nerve center at her nape, Christine could barely think. "David gets bad stress headaches. They're his."

"Let's hope they haven't lost their effectiveness," he commented as he opened the safety cap, extracted two, and held them out for her to take.

Billy Carlton's magnetism is downright dangerous, Christine thought, thankful when he released her. *Any woman allowed within a foot of the man should be issued steel-plate armor.*

She tossed the tablets to the back of her throat and sipped from the glass. Warily she glanced up at his face. "I'm okay. Why don't you go back?"

"I'd rather tuck you in." Lightly he caught her rib cage between his hands. When Christine inched away, a puzzled expression crossed his handsome features. Pain furrowed her brow. Billy gently brushed his lips across hers. " 'Night, luv."

Christine wanted to flee from the room, but instead she forced herself to walk sedately out the kitchen door. Without looking over her shoulder, she turned into the short hallway leading to her room.

As the aspirin began taking effect and the pain receded, Christine wished she could be part of the cozy circle outside around the fire. She could hear the three of them talking, laughing, singing. But she knew if she joined them, the double entendres would continue to be passed around the campfire like a hot potato.

"I could stare at the ceiling or count sheep," she muttered, dispirited, dreading the long hours of being wide awake with nothing to do.

Efficiently she completed her nighttime routine to get ready for bed. Then she walked back and forth in her room to expend nervous energy. Regardless of how she directed her thoughts, they boomeranged back to Billy Carlton.

He deliberately taunted her. Anyone with half an ear and a lick of sense could decipher the meaning behind his glib words. And yet Nick and Janelle didn't notice anything out of order. Was she going to have to keep on her toes every time they were all in the same room?

"I'd better buy another bottle of aspirin the next time we go to town," she muttered to herself. "The large size."

She stopped, pulled back the curtain at the window, and gazed outside at the full moon that seemed to be resting in the treetops. *What a waste*, she thought. *If Janelle and Nick hadn't warned me about Billy, the two of us could be . . . what? Writing another song in the middle of the forest?*

Yes, her heart sang sadly.

"No," she whispered forcefully. "He probably writes songs for his latest girlfriend the way other men bring candy or flowers. Flattering, but insincere."

The thought of Billy composing music with another woman hurt. But to believe otherwise would be insanely naïve. Nick wouldn't lie to Janelle; Janelle wouldn't lie to her. Christine was just one more note added to his staff paper.

Why couldn't she adopt an attitude of "take what you can while you can, then blow it off if it doesn't work out"? Other women did and didn't appear any the worse off than she was at this moment. Mentally she cringed at the thought. She gave the appearance of being a flighty, lighthearted, let's-have-a-good-time woman, but she didn't have the hard inner core it took to have a casual affair.

"Impulsive burned marshmallow," she grunted, uncharacteristically mixing her metaphors. Realizing Billy Carlton affected even her ability to use proper English, she let the chintz curtain slide through her fingertips.

She turned around and faced the desk stacked with hunting manuals and notebooks. Emotionally in a muddle, she decided to work off her frustrations rather than indulge them. Sitting down, she began flipping through the books.

Every one of them has pictures of wild game, she noticed. *My book needs pictures interspersed throughout the text to be authentic.* A mental image of a book cover showing a sexy woman armed with a cosmetic kit slung over her shoulder, reading *Hunting Male Homo Sapiens* with a foot planted on the chest of a gorgeous male, lifted her dark mood as her eyes filled with laughter.

The closing of the door across the hallway momentarily drew her attention away from the book. The campfire party must have ended. Soon Billy would be upstairs. She fervently prayed he wouldn't play the tune he'd composed earlier that afternoon. If he did, the sweet memories the song evoked would interfere with her work, her sleep, her vows to keep Billy smiling.

She twisted a lock of hair between her fingers, tugging it to get her mind off Billy and back to the project in front of her.

Pencil in hand she jotted down the idea to make certain she wouldn't lose it. Then she began making a list of wild animals on the left side of a clean sheet of paper. Her mind swung back to Billy Carlton when she scribbled "lion" at the bottom of the column.

"Too exotic," she said aloud, drawing a line through the word. "Not indigenous to the area the average woman inhabits."

And yet, she mused, it would be fun to pretend they did exist. She tapped the end of the pencil against her bottom lip. Erasing the scratched-out word, she rewrote it and placed an asterisk beside it as well as the other African animals.

"I'll devote one chapter to the big game hunter. No need to consult the experts on attracting the biggest game in this area," she whispered sardonically. In small neat letters she began writing: "Billy Carlton. Prime example. Awesome in the wild. Hums rather than roars like a lion, but the effect on the huntress is spine-tingling!" Inside parentheses she placed a question mark. She could research the magazines for candidates other than Billy, but this would be enough to cue her memory later on.

Next to "black bear" she wrote "Big Nick Gentry, poet." She grinned. There was nothing like starting out with the easy one. Across from "squirrel" she jotted "locate wealthy banker with chubby cheeks." Similar trait? The squirrel saved nuts; the banker hoarded money. Next to "duck" she wrote "national real estate broker." They both migrated looking for the best place to land.

Now for the tougher ones. Deer. A famous minister, she decided. The minister at the church she attended had the same kind, vulnerable eyes of Bambi.

Pheasants? Christine stared at the word for several moments. The same look she saw when one of her students reached the difficult part of a test was on her face. She turned to a picture of a pheasant.

Next year I'll have to give more open book tests.

Male pheasants were far more colorful than their female counterparts, she observed. Eyes sparkling, she chuckled and wrote "salesman."

Wild turkey? An over-the-road eighteen-wheeler!

Reversing the procedure, she wrote "construction worker." Immediately picturing their hard hats, she put "turtle" in the left column. The others—doctor, mechanic, teacher, architect—the quarry was limitless. Any proficient huntress could fill her game bag up to the legal limit.

Pausing, she reminded herself that the basic thrust of the book had to be the premise that the male of the species was out there waiting for the woman who bought a copy.

As she leaned back and stretched, pleased with what she had accomplished, she heard a noise at the window. David's squirrels? she wondered. She silently tiptoed to the light switch and turned it off. Did they still tap at his windows?

Slowly she pulled the curtain back, careful not to frighten them. Her heart lurched when she saw Billy's smile on the other side of the screen. Heart thudding, she raised her hand and waved in a dismissive gesture.

"Unhook the screen," Billy whispered.

Christine shook her head vehemently.

"Do you want me to come in the house and break your door down? Janelle and Nick would love that!"

"Get out of here! Go to bed."

"Unhook the screen."

"Shhhhhh! Janelle will hear you."

"I'm going to get *ve-ry* loud, *ve-ry* shortly," he warned. "I just want to talk."

"So? Talk."

"This would be romantic if you were in your old room upstairs and I was on a ladder. Ever been serenaded?" he teased, humming loudly.

"Janelle would hear you and push the ladder off the windowsill. You'd be picking thorns out of your backside the minute you opened your mouth," she threatened in a deliberate effort to be unromantic. The time she'd spent writing in an effort to forget Billy Carlton would be a wasted effort if he started charming her right before she climbed between the sheets. "Go away!"

He placed the palms of his hands on the outside of the screen. "I scared you, didn't I?"

"Don't be so damned proud of your prank. Laugh now, cry later," she warned.

"Put your hands up on mine," he crooned in a voice Christine easily recognized.

"No. I'm going to shut the window."

Christine felt her heart rate increase from another source of fear. Fear of touching him. Fear of giving him easy access to more than the darkened room.

"And I'm going to start singing at the top of my lungs. Have you any idea how loudly a professional singer can sing a cappella? You're about to find out."

She raised her hand to the screen. The heat from his fingers scorched her fingertips. But to restrain him from singing, she resisted the impulse to quickly draw it away.

"Don't! You'll have everybody in here!" she hissed, thoroughly provoked by his lack of discretion. After the warning Janelle and Nick had given her, she wasn't about to get caught with Billy in her room in the wee hours of the morning.

"I'm coming in. My handy-dandy pocketknife should make quick work of this old screen." Billy didn't have a knife, but Christine wouldn't know whether he did or not.

"You slit that screen and I'll split your skull!"

"Shssh," he whispered when her voice raised to its normal pitch. "Unlock the screen."

The firm command, and seeing one hand dropping to reach into his pocket, left Christine with little choice. She could let him rip a hole in the screen, which would be difficult to explain. She could let him awaken the whole damned house by singing. Or . . . she unhooked the latches.

Nervously she stepped back, glancing at the closed door. Why didn't her father put locks on the bedroom doors? Janelle might hear something and come to investigate. She had to do something to muffle their voices.

"Take off those damned glasses. Get in the bed," she ordered, hastily turning back the covers and crawling to the far side of the bed.

"Best offer I've had all day," Billy whispered obediently, tossing his glasses on the cluttered desk top before slipping in next to her.

Christine yanked the covers over both of their heads to cut down the chances of being overheard.

"Should I have taken time to remove my clothes?" Billy whispered as he began unbuttoning his shirt. "Your bed smells like lavender and sunshine."

"Don't you dare!" she yelped. "What do you want?"

"How's your headache?" Unmindful of her warning he slipped out of his shirt and shorts.

"Gone," she blurted, surprised by the change of topic and his hasty undressing. "You could have checked on my health from outside the window."

Christine slapped at his fingers when they began tracing the lace edging of her nightgown. Hearing his low chuckle answered her next question, "Why didn't you?"

"Your skin is smoother than the satin gown. Touch my chest."

"Billy Carlton, do you know what my sister is going to do to you if she walks in and finds you in my bed?"

"Join us?" he suggested outrageously, pulling her close. "You'll have to dissuade her."

Was it a groan or a moan she made? Christine honestly didn't know. Once flattened against him, her will to protest seemed far more ridiculous than enjoying the texture and fragrance of his body.

"Nice," he mumbled against her ear. "I've never snuggled head to toe under the covers."

Christine ineffectually made an effort to stop his roving hands. The last time she shivered under the bedclothing was years ago after David told a chilling ghost story around the campfire. She, Janelle, and David wound up in the same bed hiding from the all-too-real ghost.

Billy's callused fingertips lightly skimmed over her gown from shoulder blade to the gentle flair of her hips. Christine felt the hem rising, the fine sandpaper touch of his calluses against the backs of her knees.

"I want to kiss you there," he whispered. "Remember how beautiful it was in the glade? I can't get enough of the sweet music you make."

"Dammit, Billy! You can't just climb in my window and jump into my bed. So help me, I'm going to start screaming bloody murder. Janelle will get you out of my bed!"

His hands cupped the swell of her buttocks. "You don't need Janelle to protect you anymore. Leave everything to me. I can make your body need me. That's enough for now, isn't it?"

"No, Billy, I won't let you croon your way around what I know is right. Janelle said . . ." She bit her tongue to keep from lowering her pride enough to let him know what she'd been told.

"Yes?"

"Never mind." Christine whipped the covers back and scrambled to climb out, but Billy chuckled, and strong hands at her waist pulled her back. She wasn't fleeing from another mind-boggling interlude. She was trying to run from the passion slowly seeping into her blood. Better to run than regret staying.

"Christine, I need you. I'm going to make love to you tonight because you're the source of lovely, lovely music. Don't deny me. Don't fight me."

Acutely aware of the extent of his arousal pressed against her upper legs, she didn't struggle when his hands cupped her breasts. Had she subconsciously stayed up working in hopes he would notice her light and investigate?

His heady, tantalizing scent was as primitive as the second chorus of the new song he'd played. He rolled her shoulder over against the pillow. Face to face, he kissed her. His tongue thrust into her mouth, stroking a rhythm that matched another cadence, one she could feel but not hear.

"Oh, Billy," she sighed.

"Did you really think I could sleep tonight without being with you?"

He nibbled her lips, her neck, the tips of her breasts. His sensitive fingers dug into the flesh of her hip, then moved to the dark-shadowed tangle of hair between her legs. "How can you deny you want me?"

The fire inside Christine was burning for him. How could she deny it? Clutching the shoulders above her, silently demanding he raise his head and kiss her, she arched against his hand. His tongue and fingers magically blended into the same steadily increasing pace.

Billy felt her response. He withdrew his lips but kept the music playing inside his head by stroking her as though she were a cherished instrument only he could hear. But the faint notes were unclear. He withdrew his probing fingers, leaving Christine digging her heels into the bedding as she arched upward.

"Which direction should I move the gown bunched at your waist?" he asked in a husky whisper. "Down to cover you, or up?"

"Up. Touch me, Billy." She pulled the gown over her head and tossed it carelessly aside. "Touch me . . . the same way."

"How?" he coaxed. His head bent to the dark nipple, circling it first with his tongue, then sucking with mild passion.

"No, no—harder!" Her hand clasped the back of his head. "And . . . touch me!"

"Where? Here?" He nuzzled between her breasts.

Her hips arched again as she silently showed him the aching source of the liquid heat. Both of his hands covered her breasts, kneading their increasing hardness.

"Don't ask questions," she softly complained, shaking her head from side to side. "Just love me, Billy, love me."

"Christine, luv . . . hot, mellow, unbearably sweet."

His rigid tongue plunged inside, driving further complaints to the far recesses of her shrinking sanity. His hands lifted her hips. The master musician played a tune she had never heard before. He demanded intimacies as unexpected as the changes in his music. And as with his music, it was both exciting and shocking. He raised his head, his body, and smoothly moved up her length until his lips rested against the base of her neck. "Don't deny me. Give me the song I've never heard."

For long moments her mind spun close to the dizzy heights of satisfaction, only to plummet into delicious torment. Her mind cleared for a single, sharp insight. Billy, throughout the playing and the loving, was striving to fill a black void in his life. He'd been forced to become a man long before experiencing childhood. And without a childhood, emotionally he evolved like a toddler who was forced to walk without crawling. Just as the precocious toddler would suffer from a lack of coordination later in life, so did Billy. He lacked emotional balance. He needed the missing steps he'd been denied.

Christine dug her short nails into his buttocks to signal her willingness to give him what he needed. She couldn't deny him; she couldn't deny herself. She was so close to the edge of fulfillment, the slow, steady rhythm swirled Christine into ecstasy.

His lips slanted over hers as he entered her. Arching, driving himself into her softness, he felt her fingers biting into his hips as he joined her in mindless oblivion. He collapsed against her. His release was beautiful, total.

It was a long while before Billy summoned the energy to shift to her side. "I don't want to leave," he whispered, his hand cupped to her ear. He dreaded leaving. Away from her he was in a loveless world.

Christine stirred. She looped her arm loosely

around his waist. Brought back to the reality of where they were, who they were, she inched away from his warmth. He couldn't stay, but mercy, mercy . . . she wanted him to.

"You'll have to go," she replied softly.

"I will," he promised. "Once you fall asleep, I'll go upstairs."

Christine rolled on her side away from him and snuggled her backside against him. Within minutes she was lulled to sleep by the long strokes of his hand moving over her waist and hip.

In his mind, Billy recorded the pure sweet melody he'd heard. He fingered the chords of accompaniment on her hip. Certain she was sound asleep, he carefully shifted his weight off the bed. The blend of regret and wistfulness on his face couldn't be seen by anyone, but Billy felt it.

For long silent moments he stood beside her bed staring at Christine. His eyes glanced toward the door when he thought he heard a noise in the hallway. Janelle? He cocked his head, holding his breath as he stood stock-still. Christine would be horrified if her twin walked in. The silence from the hall reassured him that they hadn't been overheard.

He understood Christine's reluctance to openly flaunt sleeping with him. But he couldn't understand why she thought Janelle was perfect for him. And he couldn't understand why she looked to her twin for protection.

A tender smile flashed across his face. The lovely woman curled into a semifetal position faked the world out by outwardly appearing to be spunky, but inside she was . . . . "Soft, sweet," he whispered, "and beautiful."

As he bent down to gather up his shirt and shorts, he remembered the glasses he'd tossed carelessly on the desk. Reluctant to leave any clues for Janelle to find, he blindly felt around the cluttered desk top. He ran his fingertips over stacks of books, papers, pencils and pens, and various objects he couldn't recognize in the total darkness, but he couldn't find his sunglasses. When a couple of pencils rolled off the desk to the hardwood floor, he realized how much noise he was making. He decided to risk turning on the small desk lamp.

I shouldn't have worn them, he castigated himself silently. He didn't need them with Christine.

Cautiously he cupped one hand over the desk light. With the other hand he switched it on. His dark eyes quickly surveyed the clutter. As he reached for the glasses which had slipped between two stacks of books, he saw his initials in a star linked to a heart enclosing Christine's initials. A broad smile wreathed his face. Curious, he glanced at the chart she made. Again he saw his name. As he read her notes, the corners of his lips slowly sagged until he drew them into a harsh straight line.

He ripped the page out of the spiral notebook, mindful of the noise. He creased the sheet and stuffed it in his shirt pocket. Afraid of overreacting to the damning evidence, he snapped off the desk light instead of letting loose the bellow of rage he felt.

Silently, angrily, he stalked to the window and disappeared into the night.

CHAPTER EIGHT

By morning Billy felt raw, betrayed. To avoid contact with any of them he got up before dawn to stockpile food in his room. He wanted to nurse his wounds privately. At one point during the night he considered packing up and driving to the nearest airport. But the revenge he plotted had many sweet forms, none of which could be executed long distance.

Fair play usually dictated his actions. But Christine started the foul play with the marble game straight through to the huddled-under-the-covers play to get information for her book. She deserved anything he dished out. And he planned on giving a five-course meal of revenge.

He recalled Christine plotting to match him up with Janelle. Presently he considered fervently pursuing Janelle as part of Christine's well-deserved punishment. One flaw kept him from following that course. There were times when Janelle looked at him as though he were a cockroach on the wall and she held a can of Raid in her hand. Chances were, Janelle would sic Big Nick on him if he tried anything with her.

He wanted to go downstairs, bang on Christine's door, and demand to know what the hell she thought she was doing by including him in her book. But pride kept him in his room. Pride and fear. Could she have faked a response while she silently tallied up a scorecard about his lovemaking? Would she advise women on how to make love to a rock star? Instruct them on what to say? Coach them about his vulnerable psyche? Was she like the others who stole a piece of his soul as slickly as a professional pickpocket?

By noon Nick had pounded on his door several times. Billy told him to go away; he was working. Christine received the same reply. Let her worry and wonder!

"Hustler," he mumbled over and over. She didn't gamble with anything she valued. He should have known when she made a joke of losing David's marbles that she couldn't be trusted.

Trust.

The occasional laughter coming from downstairs irked him. The three of them sounded as happy as boll weevils in a Texas cotton patch. Little did Nick know that he, too, had been duped. Nick would explode when he discovered the deception. Subtle revenge wasn't in the poet's vocabulary. But Billy wasn't about to confide in Nick before he exacted revenge himself.

The more he contemplated Christine's deceptiveness, the more befuddled he became. *Dammit,* he silently swore, *the facts are in her own handwriting.* Repeatedly he tried to convince himself that she was a scheming, conniving bitch, but the phrase rang with a false note. Inside, something told him the hard cold facts didn't ring true.

Nothing made sense.

Christine marked time during the four days Billy the Kid holed up in his room. Nick assured both women that Billy's actions weren't unusual. His best music was often composed in total isolation.

She couldn't understand this facet of his artistic temperament. Instead of barricading herself in her room, she brought her spoof out in the open for all three of them to work on. At first Janelle voiced an objection to the preface, but when Big Nick boisterously laughed, and made Christine promise to use one of the pictures Janelle had taken of him in the woods, Janelle capitulated.

She felt frustrated by her lack of efficiency when she couldn't find the chart she'd made. She could have sworn she'd worked up a list of animals and corresponding types of men, but she couldn't find it in any of her notebooks. She reconstructed the list and gave it to her sister and Nick to read.

A strange expression crossed Nick's face when he saw Billy's name written beside the lion. Christine explained that Billy exemplified her image of a lion, but she wasn't about to stick her head in the lion's mouth by actually using him in the book. Neither Nick nor Janelle said anything, but she knew from the skeptical expressions on their faces that they didn't believe her.

The third day Christine observed drawn lines of worry etched on Nick's forehead. She questioned him, but he shrugged his massive shoulders, glanced at the ceiling, and shook his head. After lunch Nick climbed into the pickup truck he'd parked in back of the cabin and drove off without a word to either Janelle or Christine. He didn't return until late that night. Then he and Janelle went for their habitual late-night walk, and when they returned Christine thought they both could be paired with "clam" on her list. Their mouths were thin lines, and sealed shut.

The following afternoon Christine decided to enter the lion's den. She respected Billy's need for solitude, but she had needs too! She needed to see him, talk to him, touch him.

She loudly stomped up the steps. The door was open, the room empty. Glancing around her old bedroom, she noted the box of crackers and half-empty jar of peanut butter open on the desk top. Had Billy existed on peanut butter and crackers? she wondered.

Christine cast a nervous look over her shoulder. Being afraid was ridiculous, she thought. Billy wouldn't eat her alive for going into her old room. But not being too certain of his possible reaction, she crossed to the desk and busily removed the thumbtacks from the unicorn poster. If he caught her, she could readily explain that she wanted one of the mythical beasts in her room downstairs.

Don't snoop, she warned herself when her eyes strayed to the blank sheets of staff paper on the desk. But she couldn't help wondering where the masterpieces of music he'd been working on were stashed. Had she been the inspiration for another song? Christine peeked into each drawer, justifying her actions by rationalizing she played a major role in anything he'd written. Billy wouldn't mind.

After thoroughly searching his room, she was puzzled. She'd found nothing. If his work wasn't in his room, he must have it with him. As she crossed to the door she noticed that the wastebasket beneath the desk had tipped over. Out of habit, she bent down and set it upright.

In the bottom of the wastebasket she spotted a wadded ball of notebook paper. She stooped over to examine it but changed her mind. Looking for his music was one thing, but to invade his privacy by reading something he wrote and discarded was beneath her dignity.

"Dignity," Christine snorted derisively. "You're scared to death it's something you don't want to read."

Her stomach fluttered. Did Billy know she'd fallen for him? Was he contemplating a way to get out of a sticky situation with his agent's sister? A brief note would be brutal but effective. This ball of paper could be a draft of the note . . . or it could be the song.

Unable to leave the room without knowing, she decided to stoop beneath her dignity and conquer her fear.

It's my list! What's he doing with it? She turned the sheet over and saw a string of notes written on the back. Grinning, she pictured Billy climbing out the bed they'd shared and hurriedly jotting down the music he'd heard, then taking it with him.

Christine wadded the list up and did a little jig as she dropped it back in the wastebasket. There was no need to let him know how worried she'd been.

But where is he? she wondered. Not downstairs in the kitchen with Nick and Janelle. Outside, she surmised as she walked out of his room. For four days Billy had remained incommunicado, supposedly working. This time she wanted to hear his new song when they were alone, not in front of a campfire with Janelle and Nick.

Billy sprawled backward in the grassy glade. He closed his eyes to recapture the precious moments when his heart had sung joyfully. He could taste her, feel her, hear her. No, he mused, his mouth forming a sardonic smirk. He might be a fool, but he wasn't crazy. A stark-raving-mad lunatic wouldn't be able to remember each intimate detail the way he could.

His hands dug into the loose soil beneath the grass. Christine had one weakness: her twin. But he wouldn't involve outsiders in settling their problems. This was between Christine and himself. He'd find a way to get the truth out of her. Patience was the key. He'd let her think she could easily seduce him again, but this time he'd be ready . . . mentally instead of physically.

The sun, high overhead, heated the skin on his bare torso. He got to his feet and automatically headed for the icy waters of the mountain stream. He whirled around when he thought he heard twigs snapping a hundred yards behind him. The short hairs on the back of his neck prickled upward. Shrugging, he stuck his hands deep in the pockets of his navy blue shorts. He listened carefully as he started walking.

Again he heard strange sounds. Billy swung around. He removed his sunglasses and peered intently into the thick trees. Were there black bears in the area? A bobcat? He brushed the palm of his hand over the nape of his neck. What or who was following him? A tingle of fear raced up his spine.

"Who's there?" he bellowed, thinking if it were Nick, Christine, or Janelle they would join him. And if it wasn't one of them, his shouting would scare away any wild creatures.

Christine stooped behind a thick bush. The giggles threatening to spill out of her mouth were muffled by the brown beach towel she carried. Dressed in a greenish-yellow two-piece bathing suit with cutoffs over the bottoms, she hoped he wouldn't be able to spot her.

As his fingers trailed over the golden hairs on his chest to wipe off the thin film of perspiration, Christine wiped at the beads of sweat trickling into the shadowed cleavage of her breasts. The forest seemed to have taken a deep breath and held it. Nothing stirred. Christine softly blew a puff of air upward to remove her curly bangs from her forehead. Was it the summer heat, or was it observing Billy Carlton that had her blood pounding through her veins like thick streams of molten lava?

Carefully, one eye on his back, the other on where she was tiptoeing down the path, she followed him. Each time he swung around, she ducked or hid behind a tree.

His pace quickened for a few seconds, then he whirled around again. Christine remained frozen, crouching stock-still in the bushes. She now understood why a hunter wore camouflage clothing.

Second-guess your prey, she mused, remembering a line she had written that morning. *Know his habits, and be there when he arrives.*

Christine knew the path came to a fork several hundred yards farther up. If he went to the left, he'd be going back to the cabin. If he took the trail to the right, it would lead to the creek.

Most likely he'd head for the creek, she deduced. Rather than follow him when he suspected her presence, she weaved her way through the underbrush, making a beeline for the creek. She'd end up downstream from his destination, but she wouldn't stand the same risk of being caught. For the first time, Christine understood the thrill of the hunt Janelle talked about.

From the corner of his eye Billy saw Christine skulking on tiptoes off to his right. Urban guerrillas didn't belong in a mountain forest, he thought, amused by the amount of noise she made.

A wide grin spread his lips. How long had she been sneaking along behind him? Christine may have done her homework by reading manual after manual about hunting, but like the amateur hunter and the wily polar bear, the hunted could become the hunter.

Depending on his ears to detect her presence, he chuckled when he heard the branches snapping downstream from where he stood. Mentally he thanked show business for eliminating a natural tendency toward modesty. Without the slightest hesitation Billy shucked his navy shorts, leaving himself totally nude except for white bikini underwear.

He tested the temperature of the sun-dappled water with his big toe, and stood there waiting.

Patience was an easy virtue for a man who wanted to be seduced.

Christine watched him rub his torso with both hands as he slowly waded into the spring-fed water. The current swirled, pushing against the muscular calves of his legs. Billy bent at the waist to acclimate the pulse points at his wrists to the change in temperature. The vaguely familiar tune he whistled accompanied the rhythmical splashes he made as he waded deeper.

The new song? she mused.

Billy disappeared beneath the surface. Christine straightened from her crouched position behind some low bushes. Given enough time, she could sneak out of hiding and swipe his shorts. She stealthily moved toward the underbrush directly behind the point where he'd entered the creek. She gauged the distance between her protective covering and the article of clothing, keeping an eye on where he had gone under.

Seconds later, when his head didn't bob up, she began to worry. *The damned fool shouldn't be swimming by himself.* A four-day diet of peanut butter and crackers was enough to give anyone stomach cramps. Was his foot caught between the boulders in the deepest part of the pool? Christine forgot about stalking her prey and dashed to the edge of the stream.

"Where are you?" she muttered as she slipped off her canvas shoes. He'd been under too long. "Billy?"

She felt herself propelled forward before she heard, "Right behind you!"

Arms flailing as though grabbing for a sky hook, she executed a perfect belly flop.

"You rotten skunk!" she sputtered once she'd righted herself in the shoulder-deep water.

Billy stood, hands on his hips, pelvis thrust forward, laughing wickedly. "The hunted captures the hunter," he hooted, enjoying the first taste of revenge. The old adage was right. Revenge *was* sweet!

Wiping the hair out of her face, she stormed toward him. Hellbent on getting even for his underhanded stunt, she paddle-wheeled her hands, splashing him from head to foot. Billy catapulted into the water and grabbed her by the waist with one arm.

"Wanna play rough, huh?" A hand on top of her head, he dunked her face in and out of the water three times in rapid succession. "What were you going to do once you had me in your sights?"

"Shoot you, you horse's patoot!"

Billy laughed and dunked her again. Wrong answer, he thought. When her head cleared the surface he asked, "With a gun . . . or a camera?" His eyes narrowed. "Maybe you could use my picture in your book?"

Locking her arms around his shoulders to avoid any more dunkings, she laughed merrily. Billy was out of his self-imposed isolation, and in her arms. Nothing could be better!

Billy twined his long fingers in her hair, bent his knees, and let both of them sink to the bottom. Once underneath the water he ran his free hand the length of her body as though frisking her.

"You scoundrel," she spat through thousands of teeny bubbles. Ineffectually she slapped at the hand that settled over one of her breasts.

He hauled her upright as he planted his feet wide apart. "Your picture, unlike mine, isn't readily available. I'm memorizing what you look and feel like with my hands."

Her eyes sparkled with laughter at his outrageous excuse for intimately touching her.

Was she laughing at him, or with him? Billy's black eyes searched for the hidden deceit. All he saw were the golden flecks of arousal in the recesses of her velvet-brown eyes. He dodged her blows by nuzzling the side of her neck, taking love bites.

"Don't you know it's illegal to kill wild game while it's swimming? Where's your sportsmanship?" he joked.

"I'm not planning on killing you," she protested weakly, clutching his slippery skin.

"There's more than one way to kill a man. More than one way to cause pain."

He hurt, physically and mentally.

Billy turned her in his arms and carried her out of the icy stream. He stifled his inner rage long enough to carefully spread the beach towel for her to sit on. He grabbed his navy shorts and swiped angrily at the rivulets of water making her shiver.

"You have a damned low opinion of one of

us," he grimly stated. His black eyes bore into her face intently.

Christine shivered, not so much from the cold as at the mask of determination on his face. "What's wrong with you? One minute we're laughing, playing, and the next minute you're angry."

"Didn't you think you owed me the courtesy of consulting me before you put me in your book? You knew I came up here to get away from the groupies. Dammit, you're one of the few people I allow to see me without my glasses! Why, Christine? Why betray me by putting me in your book?"

She could tell by the expression on his face that he'd never believe she did *not* intend to use his picture. Nick hadn't. Janelle hadn't. Her anger simmered at the injustice.

"Supposing I did consider using your name. Is that so terrible?" Christine brushed his hand away from her jaw and sat up. Wrapping her arms around her bent legs, she rocked her head between her knees.

"Yes," he hissed. "You used me!"

She looked up, eyes blazing. "Now, wait just a minute. Since you're the one who is pointing the finger of accusation, you'd better check your own hand. Four of your fingers are pointing back in your direction. You're the one with the bag of marbles, and the late-night rendezvous routine." Angry tears collected in the corners of her eyes. Her hands made small fists as she stared at him. "Who was using whom? Do you deny you've been on a sexual smorgasbord for months? Tell me I'm different from the women in California, if you can keep a straight face and lie at the same time."

"My having been with other women justifies exploiting my name. Sorry, lady. That's a lame excuse. There haven't been any celibate popular singers since the Singing Nun retired." Billy picked up a flat rock and skimmed it across the surface of the stream to rid himself of a bit of his pent-up frustration. "Try again."

Harsh laughter grated from within Christine. "A man who uses women, then tosses them aside like dirty tissues, isn't my ideal man."

"One more crack like that and I'll show you how it feels to be used. I'm an expert. I've been used by the best in the business: agents, business managers, fans. You want an example of what it's like to be used?"

Billy pushed her on her back with both hands. His thigh held her legs down. "This is what people do to me with their eyes while I'm on stage."

His free hand homed in on the zipper of her cutoffs. "There are no caresses, no kisses, just greedy probing."

Christine grabbed at his wrist, but he had the strength of a thousand demons from inside himself. She bucked and twisted, straining to gain freedom. "Billy, don't! Your name isn't in the manuscript."

"Lies, lies, and more lies." His mouth twisted

into a satanic grin. "That's what they want me to do . . . writhe. Grind your hips. Expose everything to their greedy eyes. They love it!"

"Don't do this! Please!" Christine begged, tears gathering behind her eyelids.

"Oh, no. You can't stop. You've got obligations . . . contracts . . . you can't disappoint your fans. Now do you see why I wear the sunglasses? I'm a man; I can't let them see me cry. The glasses reflect their lasciviousness right back into their faces." He rolled on top of her as he shoved her cutoffs down. "Shall I take you the way I'm taken?"

"You can't use me this way!"

Billy threw his head back and let out a cackle of agonized laughter. "That's *my* line. But you haven't been used—yet!" When he leaned forward, saw the tears of humiliation running down her face, his desire to hurt her as he had been hurt vanished. He rolled away from her. The sharp rocks dug into his flesh, but he preferred the superficial abrasions to the stabbing pains surrounding his heart.

"Get out of here, Christine. Put me in your damned book if you have to, but *get the hell out of here!*"

His body shook from the shock of revealing himself so callously. Deep inside he knew he could never forgive himself for such cruel behavior.

CHAPTER NINE

Legs shaking, Christine managed to get to her feet. The anger blazing from Billy's coal-black eyes lit the fires of her own temper.

"You can't recognize the difference between adulation, lechery, and love," Christine hurled at him. Too irate to stop herself, she slammed her feet on his shorts. The sound of his sunglasses cracking between the sole of her foot and the pebbles added kerosene to the flames. She didn't care about his blazing anger; she was too caught up in her own. Billy the Kid needed to hear some home truths for a change instead of being pampered. "Now you have to take off your sunglasses and view the world through the eyes of an adult. You're running scared, Billy. And using me to revert back to your childhood isn't going to make you hear the music again. It's time to grow up or burn out!"

"What about you? When are you going to grow up? Grow away from your twin? Don't give advice you can't follow."

Christine scampered backward from the

hand lunging for her ankle. Tears blurred her vision, but she turned and ran. There was nothing left to say. She refused to listen to his barbed criticism. As always, she should have listened to her sister. Janelle warned her. Nick warned her. But she let falling in love get in the way of clear thinking.

A sharp rock jabbed into the arch of her foot. Hopping, limping, she burst into the clearing surrounding the cabin and practically collided with Zeke's mule. The cantankerous, long-eared animal brayed, turned, and attempted to kick Christine.

Knowing the animal's reputation for kicking and biting, Christine jumped out of the way in the nick of time. "Somebody ought to hit you square between the ears with a two-by-four," she blustered.

"I've considered doing that to you."

Instantly recognizing the voice, Christine spun around and hurled herself into her brother's open arms. "David! What are you doing here?"

"Protecting a client from my impulsive sister," he replied with a laugh as he gave her a swift hug. "Where are your shoes?"

Christine blinked back a new wave of tears. When they were kids David was always on her case about going barefoot. She knew he expected an outlandish response. "I loaned them to Billy down at the creek. He's a California-sandy-beach man, not a Colorado-mountain-goat guy."

A gruff, somewhat hoarse chuckle gurgled near her ear before she stepped back.

"You haven't quit smoking, have you," she said. She glared at the pack of cigarettes in his front pocket, and also noticed the smell of tobacco on his breath.

"And you haven't stopped getting your siblings in trouble, have you," he retorted, giving her a slight shake of the shoulders with his hands.

Christine thumped the cellophane-wrapped pack. "These can be the death of you."

His blue eyes glared down at Christine as if to say, "You're far more dangerous than cigarettes." But he didn't.

"Nick called. You giving Billy problems?" Out of habit he reached into his shirt pocket. Being around Christine for five seconds made him consider lighting up two or three rather than the usual one. His eyes narrowed as he watched Christine glance over her shoulder toward the creek. "You aren't up to something, are you?"

"Me?" she protested with feigned innocence. David would have had a fit if he'd heard the shouting match between herself and Billy. She wasn't the least bit afraid of her brother, but he did have a way of intimidating her. *Hell,* she thought, *he intimidates everybody, including his clients.*

David picked a shred of loose tobacco off his tongue.

"The ones with filters are less harmful,"

Christine suggested, much preferring to discuss his smoking habit than Billy the Kid.

"A pint-size sister with a muzzle would be a blessing too, but there isn't much chance of that happening either, is there. Okay, Sis, 'fess up. Where did you bury the body?"

"The body?"

"Hmm." He sucked smoke into his lungs hoping it would anesthetize her reply. "Your face is brick red. The same way it used to be when the three of us pulled one of the pranks you masterminded."

David knew her too well to continue the innocent facade. "He's beastly. Do you know what he said?"

"No, but I know how he'd react to you putting him in your book." He watched her Adam's apple bob up and down as she gulped in agitation. "He'd cheerfully wrap his hands around your throat and throttle you."

When Nick called him in New York, David's first question—after he'd heard about Billy sequestering himself—was, "What's Christine up to?" Nick told him about the book, but tried to reassure him she wasn't actually going to use Billy's picture or his name.

"He's paranoid about publicity, isn't he."

David blew a gust of smoke in her direction like a protective shield. "Around you we're all paranoid."

She sneaked a peek over her shoulder. David would help Billy throttle her if Billy came roaring out of the woods like a wounded lion. Pitted against his top client, she didn't have a prayer, even though she was his sister.

"I'd better go in and get cleaned up for dinner," she stated, hoping to get out of harm's way. David could explode like an unstable bottle of nitroglycerine, but once the big boom was over, he quickly calmed down.

"Go pack," David instructed. "Nick thinks you might be the good medicine Billy needed to get him composing again, but we both know you're—"

"A pill? David Mc Mahon, you haven't called me a pill in years. What makes you think I haven't changed?"

"The New York City hospital sent me a release form. Sign on the dotted line and they'll pick up the corpse and deliver it to a research center." The inflection of his voice winging upward converted the statement into a question.

"Come on, David. That was a joke! You're the one who teased me about selling your bones to get rich."

"Selling my bones is one thing; selling my *client's* bones is another," he reasoned.

"But I wasn't going—"

"Christine," David interrupted, holding his palms up facing her to stop the barrage of denials, "don't confuse me with your logic. I've made up my mind. You and Janelle write the book back home in Denver, and give Billy the peace and quiet he needs to rejuvenate himself."

"What makes you so certain you know what

Billy needs? I may be just what the doctor ordered."

"Not with your beet-red face. You probably aren't fifteen minutes away from brawling with him, right?"

"I wouldn't call it brawling," Christine argued. "More like clearing the air."

"Um-hmm." His thumb pointed toward her chest. "But I know who the major pollutant is. Using him as part of your book stinks."

"Who told you he's in the book?"

"Nick!"

The screen door slammed, and Big Nick sauntered down the steps. "Did I hear my name mentioned?"

"Did you tell David that Billy is in the manuscript?" Christine demanded indignantly.

"Forget the 'he said-she said-they said' routine," David ordered. "Get packed!"

She bellied up to him to prove he didn't intimidate her. "Look, big brother," she warned, jabbing a finger into his shoulder. "You don't boss me around."

"I never did," he agreed, flashing Nick a smile. "Remember the spankings I took when it should have been your bottom over Mom's knee? So help me, Christine, if you aren't packed in ten minutes, your ass is grass and I'm the lawnmower!"

"Your lawnmower and who else's?" she retorted belligerently.

Nick rubbed his whiskers, obviously amused by David's lack of power around his sister.

"Mine. But you have to keep her mouth away from my arm. She has jaws like a snapping turtle."

"Two big strong he-men against one puny girl?" she scoffed.

"Make that two men, one woman," Janelle volunteered from behind the screen. "The suitcases are in the Jeep, David. You haul her out to the car and throw her in the trunk. I'll let her out when we're down the road a piece."

Christine swore an oath that threatened to turn the mountain air blue. Drawing herself up to her full height, she glared at each of them individually. With as much dignity as she could scrounge up she haughtily remarked, "I won't need your assistance. I'll go peaceably."

David whispering "Get the keys before she changes her mind" brought her chin up higher.

Determined to have the last word, she muttered loudly enough for everyone to hear, "In case the prosecution hasn't noticed, a Jeep doesn't have a trunk."

"No," Janelle replied, grinning as she headed for the driver's seat. "But I remember being gagged and tied to a tree when we were kids. David, do you remember what kind of knots you and Christine used?"

Christine climbed into the vehicle. "You wouldn't dare." She looked through the windshield from one grinning face to the next. "You would."

Three heads bobbed up and down enthusiastically.

"You're N.F.," she stated indisputably.

"N.F.?" Nick repeated.

"NO FUN," Janelle and David chorused, laughing.

Nick and David stepped away from the car as Janelle started the engine and turned the wheel.

"So long, beautiful," Nick called. "I'll be in touch, Janelle."

"Send me the manuscript when you finish it," David joined in.

Once they were around the bend in the road, Christine slumped in her seat. *They ganged up on me,* she thought glumly. *Shows you blood isn't thicker than water, doesn't it. What an unexpected way to leave the cabin! One wounded lion growling and two village idiots grinning.*

"Turn around," she ordered curtly, then explained, "I can't leave without saying good-bye to Billy."

"No way. I left our address and phone number on the kitchen table. As far as you're concerned, the hunt is over."

Christine considered grabbing the keys in the ignition, but she didn't. What would she say if they did go back? *Thanks for a great time, Billy. I love you, but my own brother and sister as well as the rest of the world agree that I'm . . . a pill.*

She turned her head toward the open window, dashing away a tear with the back of her hand. *Dammit, ill-fated lovers are supposed to get to say good-bye.* In her mind she saw herself slowly walking up to Billy. He'd still have his shirt off. She'd lay her hand on his chest, take one last look at his luminous black eyes, and whisper, "So long, Billy."

Her bottom lip trembled. She closed her eyes to keep from openly bawling. And if he had any guts at all, she thought, continuing the daydream, he'd defy Nick, David, and Janelle by saying . . . . The same curse she'd used earlier interrupted the scenario. She had to be realistic. If he knew she was leaving, he'd be checking the luggage to make certain she didn't steal the bag of marbles he'd legitimately won.

Dammit, she tried to tell every one of them she wasn't going to use information or pictures of Billy. None of them believed her.

Begrudgingly she realized they had substantial grounds for doubt. But she knew she would never intentionally hurt Billy. She leaned her head back. She had hurt him. Back at the creek when he'd acted like a trapped animal and aimed for the jugular of his attacker, she'd fought back. She had to.

Vividly she remembered the thrust of his tirade.

People used him. David was probably one of them, she thought, much to his discredit. And there probably were women who watched him, thinking lecherous thoughts, but for every one of their ilk, there were thousands of women who loyally attended his concerts, bought his records, without mentally undressing him. He had to see that. Those damned glasses distorted considerably more than his vision.

She grinned as she remembered how she'd smashed them to smithereens under her foot. She remembered the good times they'd had: washing dishes, playing marbles, teasing each other . . . loving each other. The fun and games far outweighed the bitterness of their last argument.

What had he said? *Grow up yourself. Quit living in your twin's shadow.* Christine couldn't remember his exact words because she'd been livid, but she did remember the gist of what he meant.

She wedged herself into the corner of the seat to keep from being jostled each time the Jeep bucked over a pothole. Had Billy made a valid observation? Was he flinging insults or giving constructive criticism?

Janelle and David were protective of her, she thought matter-of-factly. Why? Did they protect her because she was the youngest twin? Digging beneath the superfluous obvious reply, she brutally quizzed herself: *What do you do that makes your siblings feel they have to protect you?*

Ugly, ugly, end-of-the-test type question, she brooded. She did tend to act before she thought about what she was doing. And once in a while she did get herself into bad situations.

Half an hour later, Christine couldn't add anything to the lengthy list she'd compiled. Deep in self-examination, she didn't even notice that Janelle had turned off the dirt road, and the blacktop road, or that they were on the main highway.

Flippantly she thought, *So I've got a few faults.* Major flaws, she sternly corrected. What was she going to do about them? When was she going to stop being a shadow and grow up to be a real person? When was she going to be responsible for her own actions instead of expecting Janelle or David to pull her fat out of the fire?

"How long does the silent treatment last?" Janelle asked, turning down the radio.

"I'm thinking," Christine replied truthfully. No more cutesy quibbling to avoid facing harsh realities, she promised herself.

Janelle smiled at her sister, surprised she had responded. "Thinking or plotting?"

"Dissecting myself."

"And?"

Christine scrutinized Janelle's profile. "I'm wondering if twins are one person divided in half, or two separate halves."

"Two separate wholes," Janelle answered, having asked herself a similar question years ago when she refused to dress exactly like her sister.

"Are we? We both teach. We double date

more often than we single date. We live together. We eat the same foods. We ESP each other." Christine knew this was another non-stop list. "Are we?"

Janelle swallowed the bubble of laughter in her throat when she realized Christine wasn't playing a game. She was serious. "We're both born teachers. It's what I've always wanted to do."

"Yeah, but is it what *I've* wanted to do? Remember the picture stories I wrote when we were kids?"

"Are you telling me you think we should be full-time writers? We'd starve!" Janelle blurted.

"Not we . . . I. You slipped. You said should *we* be writers," she quoted, illustrating her point.

"Okay," Janelle conceded. "You write; I'll support you by teaching."

"Why would you support me?" Christine quizzed.

"Why? Because you're my sister. Families depend on each other."

"How do you depend on me?"

Janelle pondered the question for several seconds. "You get me up in the morning so I won't be late for work."

"Get an alarm clock."

"You share the cooking and cleaning."

"You could do it all. Or eat out."

"We work together on lesson plans," Janelle countered.

Christine audibly groaned. "You're stretching the truth with that one. I come up with an idea; you work it out. Besides, two unrelated coworkers could do that. Billy was right," she acknowledged aloud. She stretched her short legs straight out, rubbing her hands over her bare legs. "I'm a twenty-eight-year-old shadow who can't exist on my own."

"Billy is an only child. He doesn't have brothers and sisters. He doesn't have anyone to depend on. You do," Janelle argued. "Don't get some dumb idea you have to strike out on your own because—"

"Sisters our age usually don't live, eat, and breathe together. Why would it be a 'dumb' notion for us to live separately?"

"Because David and I would end up visiting you in jail . . . or worse!" Janelle replied, laughing the idea off.

"Surely I can manage to keep myself from behind bars without family assistance," Christine objected strenuously. For Pete's sake, she did know right from wrong. Even if no one believed her, she did.

"I'm teasing you." Janelle cast Christine a sidelong, speculative glance. "But I hope you aren't seriously considering moving out. The house payment would be pretty stiff on my salary alone."

Obligations. Contracts. Can't disappoint the fans. Billy's words rang ominously in her ears. Could she possibly be in the same trap he was in? Would she continue to go along with what others expected of her until she burned out?

"Get a roommate to share the expenses," Christine suggested. "The new music teacher hates her apartment. Ask her."

"You're not moving out," Janelle stated emphatically. "End of discussion."

"Why?"

"Because we're family. More than family. Twins. We shared the same womb; we can share the same house!"

Christine shook her head sadly. "Maybe you're as scared as I am. Could it be you aren't so certain you're a whole?"

The question hung in silence between them for the remainder of the journey. But regardless of how difficult life was on the outside, Christine decided she had to know for herself. She had to be a complete person before she could be anything else.

It took Christine a month to locate an apartment, buy furniture, and weed through the boxes of junk she'd transferred from the house to her new home. At first, capricious as ever, she contemplated getting out on her own sooner, but she realized Janelle wasn't adjusting to the thought of sharing the house with anyone other than a close relative. They both had to make adjustments.

Janelle's moods swung from one end of the emotional pendulum to the other. One day she insisted they split the furnishings, the next she refused to let one item leave the house. She called David to enlist his help. But for once, David backed Christine. When Christine explained the whys and wherefores, he extracted a promise about sending him the manuscript, then asked to speak to Janelle again. They spent over an hour on the phone long distance.

Neither of them realized how much they had shared, from cooking utensils to toothpaste. Fortunately, they did have healthy bank accounts, or the split would have been tougher. The morning Christine was scheduled to move out, that afternoon another teacher would move in.

Christine feared she'd break down and sob as she handed Janelle the keys to the house. The twins hugged each other as though one of them were moving to the opposite end of the earth, and wasn't likely to return.

"Keep the keys," Janelle insisted. "You never know when you'll change your mind."

As Christine walked from room to room of her freshly painted, newly decorated apartment she felt proud of herself for her response. Although her throat felt constricted and the words came out shaky, she declined by saying, "Janelle, I love both you and David, but if I keep the keys, they'll change into a metal, emotional crutch. Every time I'm feeling lonely, or in need of advice, I'd use them. I'd start hunting for excuses to use them." She took the keys and pressed them into Janelle's palm, slowly closing her sister's fingers around them. "You keep them. When I'm certain I'm really, *really* a whole person, you can give them to me if you still want to."

Christine brushed a melancholy tear from the side of her cheek. The hard part was over. She'd made the break. She was . . . growing.

The sheer drapes at the window overlooking the project's pool reminded Christine of the lacy fabric of the ones in the cabin. And of course, remembering the cabin brought Billy to mind.

"You'd be proud of me, Billy," she murmured aloud.

Thoughts of Billy led her to the bedroom where she had decorated the walls with Billy the Kid posters and record jackets. At first she'd felt juvenile about putting a pop singer's picture on the wall, but she realized that the only reason she hadn't previously decorated her walls as she pleased was because of Janelle's objections.

Billy belonged here. By seeing the photographs daily, it refreshed her determination to stand on her own two feet. Openly displaying the pictures was a declaration of independence.

But there was also a fair share of bittersweet memories to contend with regarding him. She caught herself turning to the newspaper's entertainment section every day looking for news about him. At the grocery store she'd practically had to slap her hand to keep it from grabbing the Hollywood tabloids and scanning the pages for a glimmer of information. Fact or fiction, it didn't matter. Anything was better than nothing.

Amid the hectic chaos of establishing herself, the manuscript had developed into a mainstay activity. She spent every spare minute either at the library doing research, or hunched over her electric typewriter. This book was her idea, her love, and she wasn't going to quit until the manuscript was finished and presented to every publishing house in the industry. It was good material, well organized, and well written.

"Two weeks," she reminded herself aloud. The self-imposed deadline kept her mind away from wondering about where and how Billy was. Completing the book was another small way of proving her own identity. Her last conscious thought each night was directed toward imagining the cover of her book.

Dreams, however, she couldn't control. The number of times she had dreamed of parting from Billy on a friendly basis was beyond counting. She remembered one recurring dream vividly. She was sitting at her desk typing the final draft of her manuscript. Suddenly, as though she'd forgotten something important, she opened the file marked UNFINISHED BUSINESS. There in the folder was a blurred eight-by-ten, black-and-white glossy of Billy. The next morning, when she recalled snatches of the dream, she scanned the pictures on the wall, noting that that particular photo wasn't there. In each dream the image became sharper. She could distinguish the slight wave at the crown of his head. A small oval scar marred his smooth forehead. There was a tiny chip in his front tooth. With each dream his black eyes were more illuminated with happiness.

Discounting the possibility of being a bit touched in the head, Christine placed her own interpretation on the dream. Billy Carlton could hear the music. Whatever bonds had imprisoned him, and had made him unable to hear, had been broken.

CHAPTER TEN

"Hiya, baby doll. How's the famous author doing?" David teased after telling his secretary not to let anyone interrupt the long-distance call.

"David! What did you think? Will it sell? Am I going to be fabulously rich? Never mind rich, hell, just get it in print!"

Christine had impatiently waited and waited to hear from her brother. A dozen times she'd been tempted to pick up the phone and call him. But she hadn't. Her blood relationship couldn't count in this business proposition. She'd informed him of this in the cover letter she mailed with the manuscript ten days, four hours, and fifty-six minutes ago.

"I've had an offer," he replied, straining to keep from chuckling. "A hardcover publishing company is—"

"Hardcover? Nobody can afford to buy hardcover books! Can't you sell it to a paperback company so I can make a few measly bucks?"

David leaned back in his leather chair and

roared with laughter. Paperback authors would kill to get the contract that was being drawn up. "Ever hear of book clubs, libraries, bookstores? You're going to make more than a few measly bucks."

"How much?"

"Oh," he said, pausing dramatically as though figuring out the amount in his head while he heard Christine sputtering on the other end of the line, "think in the range of several thousand."

"Dollars?" Christine gasped.

"That's the usual currency, but if you'd prefer food stamps—"

"I can't imagine several thousand anything! That ain't chicken feed, is it." Jumping up and down excitedly, she dropped the phone on the floor. "I dropped the phone. Don't hang up! Don't hang up!" she shouted.

"Calm down, Christine," he said, a bit excited himself. Who would have thought Christine had it in her to come up with such a gem of a book? He felt like kicking himself for not recognizing talent when it was right under his nose, or foot, as the case often was.

"I'm here . . . pinching myself to make certain I'm awake. You wouldn't kid me about this, would you? You really sold the book?" Peals of joyous laughter gurgled out of her throat when he confirmed the reality.

"Incidentally, thanks for including the permission rights for the photographs. The only one you missed getting is Nick's. How come?"

"Agents are supposed to be smart; you figure it out. Nick verbally agreed. That's sufficient, isn't it?" Christine answered sharply. Did he think she was in daily contact with Nick? Didn't he realize she'd prided herself on not contacting Billy in any way, shape, or form?

"Don't bite my arm off. I merely asked. He'll be at the concert tonight. Why don't you track him down then?"

"What concert? Where?" she quizzed, her heart pounding faster, her blood rushing to her ears.

"Billy's ending a concert tour in Denver. Don't you read the papers?" David asked, surprised by her ostrichlike manner regarding Billy Carlton. Hell, he hadn't bothered to send her tickets because he was certain Billy or Nick would.

"Billy? Here?" Sinking to the floor, her legs no longer able to take the barrage of surprises, she put her head between her knees to ward off the sensation of feeling faint.

"It's his first major concert in Colorado. Christine? Are you okay?" He couldn't tell whether she was quietly crying or laughing.

She was doing both. "I'm fine. In shock, I guess. Can you get tickets? No, never mind. You're my agent. This is business." For the life of her she couldn't string more than three words together. "I'll get the signature."

"Don't do anything—"

"Dumb?" Christine glared at the receiver,

then cooed, "Writers are notoriously eccentric."

"Uh-oh," he groaned, recognizing the devilish tone of her voice. "I'll have tickets at your apartment within the hour. I'll arrange for Nick to come by personally to deliver them." Those were promises he'd have to break records to keep, but Christine would shatter into a hundred crazy pieces when she heard Billy's new style.

"Don't bother. I'm capable of getting my own tickets, thank-you-very-kindly!" Christine banged the phone down to disconnect the line, then tossed the receiver on the floor to prevent David from calling back.

"I sold a book!" she shouted. "Billy's in Denver!" The two phrases chased round and round in her head, coming out strung together, "Billy's-in-Denver-I-sold-a-book!"

Laughing, crying, pounding her thighs, wiping her eyes, raising her hands in the clamped victory sign, she carried on completely uninhibited in the privacy of her own apartment.

"Got to get a ticket!" she screamed.

Unable to coordinate her legs, she crawled into the bedroom to the desk where she stored the telephone books. Frantically she searched for a ticket agent's number. Repeating the number, she pulled the phone off her desk and punched the buttons.

"No dial tone! No nothing!" she squawked, banging the receiver on the carpet as though Ma Bell had betrayed her in a moment of dire need. The bleeping tone signaled a phone off the hook. By the time she scrambled to the other phone, she forgot the number of the ticket agent.

"Settle down. You're going to go stark raving crazy if you don't. Take deep breaths." She sucked air into her lungs swiftly, quickly. "Oh, no! I'm hyperventilating!"

She flopped back on the floor by the phone. *Deep breath. One. Two. Three. Exhale. Deep breath. Call Janelle. Get her over here. One. Two. Three. No! Can't! Can take care of myself.* Again and again she repeated the procedure until her breathing returned to a near normal state.

Determined to keep calm, she picked up the hall phone and replaced it on the shelf. Slowly she walked into her bedroom. Clenching and unclenching her hands to steady the shaking, she dialed the number.

"I'd like tickets to the Billy the Kid concert," she requested when someone answered.

"Sorry. It's been sold out for over a week," the voice on the other end of the line droned as though tired of hearing the same request.

"There must be something available," Christine insisted.

"Sorry."

"But I must get a ticket!"

"You and fifty percent of the women in Denver who waited until the last minute."

Christine heard the agent's sniff of annoyance. "Never mind. I'll think of something."

Hanging up the phone, she gnawed at her bottom lip. The phone started to ring. Christine jerked the cord out of the wall. No way was she going to let David solve the problem.

But how? Think! Get those creative juices flowing!

She looked up at the collage of album covers and posters on the wall for inspiration. He had to be staying somewhere in town. A hotel, she thought gazing at his black, bedroom eyes. Determined not to call David, she let her fingers do the walking. She dug the Yellow Pages out of the bottom of the drawer.

Half a teeth-grinding hour later, after listening to twenty hotel operators practically laugh in her ear, she hung up the phone. Either he wasn't staying at a hotel, or the hotel wasn't about to admit he was there.

Christine walked to the closet and pulled out a pair of lilac-colored slacks with a matching top. As she changed clothes she gave herself a pep talk on fortitude, perseverance . . . and eccentricity. One way or another she would close the unfinished business file. She'd say a final good-bye without interference from her family.

Traffic around the convention center reminded her of buzzards circling their intended prey. Frustrated, she illegally parked her car in a tow-away zone. It was four o'clock, she noted, running toward the empty outside ticket windows.

"Scalpers! I'll get a ticket from a scalper," she

mumbled. Her dark head pivoted from side to side without sighting anyone who faintly resembled a hawker.

Where there is a will, there is a way, she reminded herself. Christine paced in front of the locked front entrance. *Can't get in the front door? Try the back door!*

She tried every door along the way. "Locked tighter than a tomb," she grumbled, giving a side entrance doorknob a resounding jerk.

"Hey, lady," she heard from behind her. "You can't get in until tonight."

Christine turned, hatching up a scheme in the hundred yards between herself and the armed guard. Smiling her most brilliant smile, she opened the flap of her purse, pretending to search for an identification card.

"Press," she announced regally. "I'm here to do a story."

"Gotta press card?"

Sending a silent prayer heavenward, Christine folded a twenty-dollar bill and clamped it underneath her teacher's identification card. The guard might not be able to read the card, but he'd recognize green currency.

The money disappeared into his pocket as he handed the card back. "Down the hallway and turn left. The dancers are prancin' around on the stage."

Unable to resist, Christine grabbed his ruddy cheeks between her palms and planted a smacking kiss on his cheek. "Thanks!"

Barely twenty feet down the hall she heard

him chuckle. "Yer welcome, teach! Don't tell how ya got in, ya hear?"

She gave him the okay signal with her thumb and forefinger. Heart pounding, feet matching the muffled beat she could hear coming from the bowels of the building, Christine ran to the darkened side entrance on the ground floor. Bright lights bounced their beams around the empty seats; floodlights lit the stage where dancers followed the lead of the choreographer who was shouting out numbers as they danced to music throbbing from the speaker system.

Christine crouched down into a seat near the aisle several rows back from the stage.

She recognized the song from one of Billy's musical videos. In fact, it was one of the songs she and Janelle had taped and used to teach dance steps to the school's cheerleaders. Her eyes widened as she watched it performed live. Caught up in the performance she momentarily forgot the reason behind sneaking inside the auditorium. The dancers began building a human pyramid.

Billy should be on stage, she silently wailed. At the end of the song he was supposed to catch the top dancer when she jumped down. Christine's eyes scanned the small groups of people standing in front of the stage. Not one of them had Billy's platinum-blond hair.

Dammit, security would be too tight for her to get in tonight! This was her one and only chance.

A beam of light from overhead bounced rhythmically on the unoccupied seats around her. Christine ducked to the floor like an escapee in a prisoner of war movie. The music abruptly ended. Had they seen her? Intent on not being caught, she slithered on her belly under two rows of seats and crawled toward the center aisle. Mentally she pictured the worst thing possible: David and Janelle at the jail posting bond.

"Is she hurt?" echoed from high above.

Who? Christine wondered, not able to raise herself high enough to see.

"Twisted ankle," came from the other end of the auditorium. "Call the understudy."

"Will do."

Christine flattened herself on the cold concrete floor when she heard running footsteps in the aisle.

"Think short. Billy has to be able to catch her when she jumps."

"Hey, Charlie. Can one of the other girls be switched? There seems to be a shortage of small dancers on call."

I'm short! I know the dance steps! This is my chance!

"I'm here!" she shouted, jumping to her feet. "I can do it!"

"What the hell?" the stage director shouted. "Get the guards!"

"No!" Christine shouted. She rushed down the rows screaming, "Billy knows me!"

"Get her out of here! Turn up the house

lights!" the director curtly instructed. "Damned crazy woman!"

Christine's legs seemed to be paralyzed when she saw a group of men from in front of the stage start toward her. "No! I'll leave! It was a mistake!"

The house lights came on, shocking her eyes and her legs into instantaneous action. She wasn't about to be trapped and hauled off to jail.

She turned toward the back of the auditorium. Tears blurred her vision. She'd failed. She gave it her best shot, but she wouldn't be able to say the good-bye she'd dreamed of.

Her feet faltered. Good-bye? *Good-bye?*

She had smuggled herself into the theater to say good-bye? Volunteered to jump from the top of a human pyramid just to land in Billy's arms to say good-bye?

She wasn't here to say good-bye. She loved Billy Carlton. Loved him enough to risk being tossed in jail. Enough to risk anything to be in his arms.

She glanced over her shoulder and saw a man dressed in a policeman's uniform coming up the aisle after her. Head turned toward the stage, she plowed into the man who stepped into her path.

"Playing tag?" she heard as she struggled to break away and get her balance at the same time. The low crooning tone mingled with laughter was instantly recognizable.

"Billy!" she squeaked, wrapping her arms around his waist.

"I have her," he shouted to the men who were only a few feet away, prepared to protect the star of the show. His black eyes brimmed with the happiness she'd seen in her dreams. "I do have you, don't I?"

"Yeah, I'm IT," she quipped, laughing, hugging him, feeling higher than she did when David told her she'd sold the manuscript.

"Back off, men," Big Nick roared, breaking through the knot of men clustering around them. "She's a wild woman. She bites!"

"Nick!" Christine pulled herself away from Billy's arms. "Give me a hug."

Roaring with laughter, a beardless Nick, one she hadn't recognized, swung her round and round in a rib-crushing hug.

"Where's your beard?" she asked when her feet touched the ground.

"I shaved it off before we left the cabin," he announced, showing off his profile by turning his head from side to side.

Billy pulled her back against himself. "We're going to the hotel, Nick. Can you cover for me here?"

"Don't I always? See you later, Christine," he replied with a bear-who-caught-a-trophy-sized-salmon grin on his face.

Twining their fingers together, Billy towed a giggling Christine who had to jog to keep pace with his long-legged stride. Outside, Christine laughed merrily when she saw his waiting limousine.

"Outrageous display of opulent wealth," she teased with mock sternness. With a giggle she leaned against his shoulder to add, "Where do I get one?"

Inside the silver Lincoln with darkened windows, her dark eyes flecked with gold, she openly admired Billy. She couldn't think of anything to say that would make sense. She remembered the thousand and one ways she'd thought of to say good-bye, but she had nothing to express the joy of saying hello.

Billy grinned as he saw the smudges of dirt on the knees of her slacks, her forearms, the tip of her pert nose. Reaching into the back pocket of his slacks, he pulled out a handkerchief and dabbed at her dirty face.

"You look like a lovable street urchin," he mumbled, tongue-tied himself. Unable to resist, he gently folded her into his arms as the driver pulled out into the traffic.

"I crawled into the auditorium on my hands and knees," she mumbled into the crook of his neck. She realized she would have willingly crawled over a bed of hot coals to get to him.

Billy chuckled. He hauled her onto his lap wishing he could tuck her into his pocket to keep her close at all times. "I've missed you."

"Me, too," she whispered, peppering his neck with tiny kisses.

"I had David keep me posted on what you were up to," he confessed. "You're living alone.

And you're about to become a world-famous author."

Squirming on his legs, trying to get as close as possible, she nipped the lobe of his ear. A spark of mischief lit her eyes. "You'll love the cover. Big, sassy lion with the face of a singing angel." Billy rolled his eyes, his teeth playfully sinking into her neck as his hands tickled her ribs. A bubble of laughter floated into his ear. "You're being vain! I told you I wouldn't use *your* picture."

"Selective listening on my part. I should have listened," he agreed solemnly.

"And you should have called me . . . rather than my brother," she added.

"He's had my phone numbers in case of an emergency . . . such as you finding a handsome, witty, charming—"

Christine ended his litany with a hard kiss. "Impossible."

"Well, I figured you'd hang up on me unless I made a few radical changes. But I'd have been on your doorstep tonight if you didn't show up in the front-row seats I reserved for you."

Christine leaned back in his arms, startled. "You arranged for a ticket?"

"Uh-huh. It's being delivered with several dozen red roses to your apartment." His black eyes locked on her rounded lips. "A *man* courts his woman with flowers instead of bags of marbles."

For the first time she noticed . . . he wasn't wearing sunglasses. Her fingers stroked his temple where the frames should have been. "I had some growing up to do myself. Could we go to my apartment?"

He pressed a button on the armrest, then instructed the driver to go to Christine's address.

"Luv, you can take me anywhere," he crooned, lowering his lips to hers. "I love you," he mouthed silently on her lips. She was pliant in his arms. He twisted their bodies until he lay beneath her on the plush velour backseat.

Christine eloquently expressed how much she loved and missed him with a kiss of great tenderness and longing. The tip of her tongue traced the edge of his teeth. She felt the slight chip she'd seen in her dream photo.

"It's crazy," she whispered, "but I knew you'd chipped your tooth."

"Carelessness. I was thinking of you as I sang, and I knocked the steel rim of the microphone against my front tooth." His tongue tracked over the uneven edge.

Remembering the small oval scar, she ran her fingertips over his forehead under the lock of hair. She grinned against the side of his mouth when she found it. "A scar?"

"Hmm. Measles when I was a kid," he answered. His hands skimmed over the side of her breast, the swell of her hip. "Please tell me your apartment is fairly close."

She heard the hoarse tones in his voice, felt the hard delineation of him against her thigh.

"I've never made love in the backseat of a limo," she whispered suggestively.

Billy groaned. Possessively he squeezed her hips with his hands as he fervently sought her lips. His tongue plunged into the sweet softness of her mouth. Much as he wanted her, he wasn't going to allow himself to get carried away in the backseat of the car. He touched the fullness of her breast as he visualized how they looked, how they tasted. The small whimpering sounds coming from Christine threatened to shatter his resolve to conduct himself as an adult, not a kid.

"We're here, sir," crackled from the small speaker behind the backseat.

Frustration mingled with relief as he helped Christine sit up. "Lead the way, I'll follow," he gruffly requested.

Christine hopped out of the limo, impatiently waiting while Billy told the driver to return in two hours. She knew he had a performance at nine o'clock, but a couple of hours wasn't enough time. *How much time do I want?* she silently asked herself. A lifetime? Eternity, she firmly answered, blowing away any lingering images of giving Billy a fond, friendly farewell.

Billy followed her into the modern apartment building. He took the key from her hand and unlocked the door. She waited expectantly for him to enter. Grinning, he plunked the keys back in her purse and swung her up in his arms.

"You're not looking at the apartment," she teasingly reprimanded as he carried her through the living room with his eyes wavering from hers only long enough to get a feel of the place.

"What I'm seeing is beautiful, but I'm anxious to see if you plastered unicorns on the bedroom walls," he complimented and teased at the same time.

"A different sort of mythical beast is in there," she warned softly, pointing him in the right direction. "One I've dreamed of constantly. One who qualified as the centerfold picture in my book but who was too precious to share with any other woman."

Billy stood in the doorway of the bedroom looking at the myriad photographs of himself. "Me?" he choked out emotionally. "I've been in your room the whole time we've been apart?"

"In my room, in my thoughts, in my heart. I love you, Billy Carlton," she whispered.

He crossed the room. After he'd lowered Christine to the Oriental silk coverlet, he kneeled beside the bed holding her hand in his.

"I loved the spunky girl at the creek who made me take off my glasses to take an unobstructed look at the world. Do you know what I saw?"

Mutely Christine shook her head.

"A kid. Not you, me. Not being able to see the various shades of love all around me killed my soul, and eventually the music inside my head. The minute I told you to get the hell away from me, I knew I'd made the biggest mistake of my life. But, gut level, I knew you'd end up hating me unless I could see myself without the glasses."

He pressed her hand between both of his as he continued thoughtfully, "I discovered there are shades of love just as there are shades of colors. No two colors, no two kinds of love are the same. The next time I performed I watched the audience. I prepared myself for the worst, but it wasn't there. Maybe, subconsciously, the shade of love the audience gave me is what kept me going. I don't know."

He raised his black velvet eyes to search her face as though wondering whether or not he was making sense.

"Go on," Christine encouraged, drawing the back of his hand against the side of her cheek.

"I felt smothered by the kind of love my parents had given me. But my vision of them has become less distorted too. Have you ever been in a room decorated in a solid, bright color? At first the room appeals to your senses, then with time you start to feel claustrophobic. That's how I felt. I had to get away from them." Unexpectedly he grinned. "Now I can be around them in short doses and love them in return."

Christine smiled.

"And there's a different shade of love I feel for Nick. Again, a completely different hue."

The callused pad of his index finger followed

the line of her jaw to the corner of her lips. "What I feel for you is another color altogether. Actually a blend of colors. Yellow. Red. Green. Pure white. I think of a whimsical shade of yellow when I hear you laugh. When we make love a thread of red and green braids together. Passion and serenity. But there is an unspoiled aura of white around you." He laughed huskily. "Similar to streaks of lightning. You certainly made the hair frizz on the back of my neck when you told me to take off the glasses and see the world."

Christine propped herself up on one elbow. Stroking the trimmed short hairs, she held his beloved face against her own. "Kids thrive on a here-and-now kind of love, but we've found something better." She sighed peacefully. "Can a famous author find eternal happiness with a performing artist?"

Billy framed her face between his palms and saw the impish gleam in her eyes. "Is that a proposal?"

She used one hand to slowly unbutton her blouse. "You're going to have to buy a copy of my book. The last line is 'Pet and love the captured prey until he learns to say . . . I do. See you at the wedding!'"

Billy Carlton alias Billy the Kid:
A New Dimension for the Fans of
Billy Carlton.
The audience shrieked their enthusiasm for his foot-tapping, hand-clapping versions of a

variety of award-winning selections. Billy reached an all-time Rocky Mountain high by introducing his bride-to-be, local author Christine Mc Mahon. The program peaked with a show-stopping medley of "So Long," "Shades of Love," and "Forever." *Ed. Note:* This crusty, hard-nosed reporter wiped his eyes during the medley. Christine Mc Mahon is Billy Carlton's "Forever."

—*Rocky Mountain Times*

You can reserve November's Candlelights <u>before</u> they're published!

- ♥ You'll have copies set aside for *you* the instant they come off press.
- ♥ You'll save yourself precious shopping time by arranging for *home delivery*.
- ♥ You'll feel proud and efficient about organizing a system that *guarantees* delivery.
- ♥ You'll avoid the disappointment of not finding *every* title you want and need.

ECSTASY SUPREMES $2.75 each

- ☐ 97 **SWEETER TOMORROWS**, Kit Daley 18425-8-18
- ☐ 98 **MILLION-DOLLAR LOVER**, Blair Cameron . . . 15634-3-52
- ☐ 99 **A GLIMMER OF TRUST**, Alison Tyler 12913-3-10
- ☐ 100 **TOO CLOSE FOR COMFORT**, Ginger Chambers 18740-0-16

ECSTASY ROMANCES $2.25 each

- ☐ 378 **GOLDEN DAYS**, Kathy Clark 13170-7-40
- ☐ 379 **LOVE IS ALL THAT MATTERS**, Tate McKenna . 15006-X-37
- ☐ 380 **FREE AND EASY**, Alison Tyler 12682-7-35
- ☐ 381 **DEEP IN THE HEART**, Donna Kimel Vitek 11784-4-18
- ☐ 383 **THAT SPECIAL SMILE**, Karen Whittenburg . . 18667-6-23
- ☐ 383 **ALWAYS KEEP HIM LAUGHING**, Molly Katz . . 10331-2-18
- ☐ 384 **A WHISPER AWAY**, Beverly Wilcox Hill 19576-4-13
- ☐ 385 **ADD A DASH OF LOVE**, Barbara Andrews . . . 10017-8-35

At your local bookstore or use this handy coupon for ordering:

Dell DELL READERS SERVICE—DEPT. BR818A
P.O. BOX 1000, PINE BROOK, N.J. 07058

Please send me the above title(s). I am enclosing $_____ (please add 75¢ per copy to cover postage and handling). Send check or money order—no cash or CODs. Please allow 3-4 weeks for shipment. CANADIAN ORDERS: please submit in U.S. dollars.

Ms Mrs Mr _____

Address _____

City State _____ Zip _____

Candlelight Ecstasy Romances

306	ANOTHER SUNNY DAY, Kathy Clark	10202-2-30
307	OFF LIMITS, Sheila Paulos	16568-7-27
308	THRILL OF THE CHASE, Donna Kimel Vitek	18662-5-10
309	DELICATE DIMENSIONS, Dorothy Ann Bernard	11775-5-35
310	HONEYMOON, Anna Hudson	13772-1-18
311	LOST LETTERS, Carol Norris	14984-3-10
312	APPLE OF MY EYE, Carla Neggers	10283-9-24
313	PRIDE AND JOY, Cathie Linz	16935-6-23
314	STAR-CROSSED, Sara Jennings	18299-9-11
315	TWICE THE LOVING, Megan Lane	19148-3-20
316	MISTAKEN IMAGE, Alexis Hill Jordan	15698-X-14
317	A NOVEL AFFAIR, Barbara Andrews	16079-0-37
318	A MATTER OF STYLE, Alison Tyler	15305-0-19
319	MAGIC TOUCH, Linda Vail	15173-2-18
320	FOREVER AFTER, Lori Copeland	12681-9-28
321	GENTLE PROTECTOR, Linda Randall Wisdom	12831-5-19

$1.95 each

At your local bookstore or use this handy coupon for ordering:

Dell DELL BOOKS BR818B
P.O. BOX 1000, PINE BROOK, N.J. 07058-1000

Please send me the books I have checked above. I am enclosing $ _____ (please add 75c per copy to cover postage and handling). Send check or money order—no cash or C.O.D.'s. Please allow up to 8 weeks for shipment.

Name _____

Address _____

City _____ State Zip _____

MARIANNE HARVEY

Know the passions and perils, the love and the lust, as the best of the past is reborn in her books.

- ___ THE DARK HORSEMAN 11758-5-44 $3.50
- ___ GYPSY FIRES* 12860-9-13 2.95
- ___ GYPSY LEGACY* 12990-7-16 2.95
- ___ STORMSWEPT* 19030-4-13 3.50

*Writing as Mary Williams

At your local bookstore or use this handy coupon for ordering:

Dell DELL READERS SERVICE—DEPT. BR818C
P.O. BOX 1000, PINE BROOK, N.J. 07058

Please send me the above title(s). I am enclosing $_____ (please add 75¢ per copy to cover postage and handling). Send check or money order—no cash or CODs. Please allow 3-4 weeks for shipment.
CANADIAN ORDERS: please submit in U.S. dollars.

Ms./Mrs./Mr._____

Address_____

City/State_____ Zip_____